MOLLY MOON

Monster Music

Georgia Byng made her debut as a talented new children's author with *Molly Moon's Incredible Book of Hypnotism*. This exciting and funny adventure starring Molly Moon, an orphan who discovers a hidden talent for hypnotism, was a runaway success. It was published in thirty-six languages and forty countries, and won the Salford, the Stockton and the Sheffield Children's Book Awards. Its sequels, *Molly Moon Stops the World*, *Molly Moon's Hypnotic Time-Travel Adventure*, *Molly Moon, Micky Minus and the Mind Machine* and *Molly Moon and the Morphing Mystery*, have firmly established Molly as a favourite with readers all around the globe.

Georgia Byng grew up in a large, noisy family in a house in Hampshire. She now lives in London with the artist Marc Quinn and her three children. Georgia loves to travel, whether it's flying off to India to research ideas for a new book or whizzing around London in her little electric car.

Visit www.meetmollymoon.co.uk for hypnotic fun, ringtones and games!

MOLLY MOON

and the
Monster Music

Georgia Byng

MACMILLAN CHILDREN'S BOOKS

First published 2012 by Macmillan Children's Books

This edition published 2013 by Macmillan Children's Books
a division of Macmillan Publishers Limited
20 New Wharf Road, London N1 9RR
Basingstoke and Oxford
Associated companies throughout the world
www.panmacmillan.com

ISBN 978-0-330-47106-0

1 3 5 7 9 8 6 4 2

A CIP catalogue record for this book is available from
the British Library.

Printed and bound by CPI Group (UK) Ltd, Croydon CR0 4YY

For Jennie –

life is very special

whenever you are around.

I couldn't have asked

for a better mum.

Chapter One

Molly Moon sat alone at a teak table on a hotel balcony overlooking a town in Ecuador. In front of her was a square. A cream stone church stood on the opposite side of this. Grand old whitewashed buildings flanked its two other sides. Trees, flowerbeds and a fountain decorated the paved open spaces between.

On a tray in front of Molly was her breakfast, her favourite food – tomato-ketchup sandwiches on white bread – and beside them a pot of tea. On her lap lay a spiral-bound notepad.

Molly sucked her pen, not realizing that its ink was dying her lips and mouth blue. So far she had written:

Name: Molly Moon (after the Moon's Marshmallow
    box I was found in as a baby).
Age: 11.

Born: In a hospital in Briersville, England.

Looks: Curly brown hair, potato-shaped nose, closely set green eyes, messy, thin, clumsy.

Grew up: In a filthy, disgusting, horrible, revolting, cold, falling-apart orphanage called Hardwick House.

Orphanage Siblings: Rocky (also aged 11), my closest person; lives in Briersville with me.

Also: Gemma (8), Gerry (8), Jinx (6), Ruby (6) – all lovely, but they live in Los Angeles now.

Other Orphanage Siblings: Hazel, Gordon, Roger, Cynthia, Craig . . . This lot wasn't very nice to me when I was growing up but maybe they have changed. They live in LA now too.

Living in Briersville with me and Rocky are . . .

1 Real sibling: Micky – TWIN.

2 New adopted brother: Ojas (from India).

3 Parents: Primo Cell and Lucy Logan. Didn't know until last year.

4 Forest: a nice old hippy.

5 Petula our brilliant black pug. She is the coolest dog ever – has a funny habit of sucking stones.

Home address: Briersville Park, England. Big posh house – completely the opposite to the orphanage.

School: Not much good at anything but . . .

Skills: Hypnotizing, time stopping (only if I have one of the special clear crystals), time travelling (as long as I have the red and green crystals), morphing (changing into animals or humans that I can see), mind reading (shouldn't really write this down as I don't want anyone to know).

Molly paused and sucked her pen again. Then she clipped it on to her pad and took a bite of her ketchup sandwich. When she took it away from her mouth she noticed that the bread was blue.

'Urgh! Look, Petula! Weird bread!'

Petula had just trotted out of Molly's bedroom. The pug scratched herself behind her collar and looked up. Cocking her head, she gave a little whine, but of course Molly couldn't understand her.

'Is Micky up?' Molly asked. Micky often slept in later than Molly.

Petula scratched her chin. Molly looked over what she had written. Her life looked fantastic on paper. Hypnotizing, stopping time, time travel, morphing, mind reading. But no doubt Lucy and Primo, her 'new' parents, would make her, Rocky, Ojas and Micky have regular school lessons when she got home. There would be no encouragement for her to use her special talents. In fact, Rocky and Ojas had probably started work already. Molly remembered that Lucy had promised she'd call today with details of Molly and Micky's flight back home from Ecuador.

'Petula, you're so lucky.' She rubbed the glossy black fur on Petula's neck. 'I mean, it might be nice to have parents who care, but mine are so . . . so controlling.'

Yes, there definitely was a downside to having parents.

They were bossy. Molly knew that that was the deal most kids got, but she still resented it. Molly, Micky, Rocky and Ojas weren't like normal kids – Micky had grown up in the future, Ojas was from the past and she had her weird and wonderful skills. Even Rocky was reasonably good at hypnotizing people using just his voice. They were definitely different.

Fuelled by this sense of injustice, Molly decided to morph. She looked around for a creature to morph into. Petula looked up.

'Don't worry, Petula, I'm not going to morph into you.' Molly laughed. Petula cocked her head questioningly. 'You're worried I won't be able to get back to myself, aren't you? Well, don't be. It's like riding a bike. Once you learn, you never forget.'

With that, Molly began to focus her mind. Petula watched. She could tell Molly was up to something because of the look of concentration on her face. And then there was a BOOM and Molly disappeared, leaving nothing but a pile of clothes.

Petula looked about.

A bird on a telephone wire strung high across the square flew towards her and landed on the balcony where it began flapping its wings. Petula brushed the air with her paw to show that she knew the bird was Molly and then she barked. The bird took off, swooped and dived above the square, then landed back on the balcony again. A minute later Molly suddenly materialized in different clothes, black jeans and a red T-shirt, while the bird sat on the balcony rail recovering from the shock of having its body and mind taken over and then getting them back again.

'That was a cinch!' Molly beamed at Petula. 'Flying is so cool. Maybe, Petula, in England, when the tutor arrives, I can just morph into any animal or insect that's nearby. I mean they can't stop me doing that, can they? They can't *make* me do schoolwork.' A worried look crossed Molly's face. 'Actually I suppose they can.'

Petula watched. A bitter smell caught her attention. It was coming from Molly's bag. It was a horrid smell, like rotten lemons with a touch of electricity that made her nose tingle. Petula wondered what was causing it. Then she was distracted as Micky plodded out of his room.

Molly's twin brother was still half asleep, his skinny frame clad in baggy pyjamas. His brown curly hair, a bit shorter than Molly's, was stuck to one side of his head and his cheek bore indentations from his pillow.

'Feels like a hippo slept on me,' he mumbled. 'What time is it?'

'It's about nine thirty. You were up late last night.'

'I know. That for me?' He lifted a silver dome off a plate of scrambled eggs and tomatoes. 'Nice. Yes. I was up with ze boyz.'

'What boys?'

'The three Japanese boys.' Micky sat down. 'The ones staying here. They're in a band. They're playing tonight. Want to see them? They're superstars in Japan. Oh, I

5

forgot – we'll probably be on a plane by then. Has Lucy rung yet?'

Molly shrugged. 'No. Should do soon.'

'Did you pick up the passports from the concierge lady?'

'Yup.' Molly poured herself a cup of tea and took a gulp. She reached for a canvas bag under her chair and felt inside it for a pouch where she kept special things. She dropped the pouch on the table and unzipped it.

'Yours, mine,' she said, dealing out the two passports. Then she flipped them both open and compared pictures. 'You look sweet! Like a little scarecrow boy!'

Micky nodded resignedly.

Next Molly tipped a very large gold coin out of the pouch. It had a raised musical note embossed on one side and its edges were crosshatched. She took another sip of her tea and picked up the coin. It had belonged to a horrible, cruel woman, whom Molly and Micky had recently had the misfortune to meet. Luckily they wouldn't be seeing her again. But Molly wouldn't forget her.

The woman's name had been Miss Hunroe. She'd had a penchant for beautiful objects and had many collections of wonderful things, from great works of art to remarkable pieces of furniture and valuable instruments. This coin had been one of her favourite things, something Miss Hunroe had carried with her always. Just before she disappeared, she had dropped it and Molly had found it. So it now belonged to Molly. She turned it over in her hand. It was heavy. Solid gold.

'I *love* this coin,' she said. 'Why does gold seem so nice?'

Molly tried to roll the coin along her fingers as she had seen Miss Hunroe do.

'Makes you feel safe and secure,' said Micky, through a mouthful of eggs. 'You know that, if you ever needed to, you could melt a bit of that coin and buy food. It's magic stuff, gold. Even if there were mountains made of it and even if there was so much of it that buildings could be covered in it, I'd still think it was magic.'

'I'm not melting it down,' said Molly, running her finger around the grooved edge of the coin. 'This is extra special. It makes me feel good. Powerful.'

Micky laughed.

'No, it does!' said Molly, slightly irritated by Micky. She stroked the coin's embossed note. 'No wonder Hunroe kept it with her all the time.'

Just then the phone went. Molly carefully put the coin back in its pouch and walked through the heavy wooden doors to answer it. She threw herself on to the sofa. For some reason she had started to feel rattled. Maybe she had got up too early. It was because of this, she told herself, that on hearing Rocky's voice she was in a mood.

'Oh, hi. So, you've rung to tell me when Mr and Mrs You'd-Better-Do-This-Or-Else want us to come home?'

Rocky said something.

'Well, I can't be nice, Rocky, because, you know, I'm really annoyed. I mean, we don't actually *need* to come home. I don't want to have lessons from some stupid tutor. Have you ever noticed that the school word "term" is the same word that's used for time spent in prison?'

On the other end of the line Rocky said something else. '. . . No, just because they're my blood parents doesn't mean they have a right to control me like some sort of remote-control toy. I should never have wished so much for parents. You and me and Micky and Ojas could easily get by without them.' She paused as Rocky spoke. 'I am not ranting,' she replied. 'Tomorrow?' Rocky spoke again. '. . . What? . . . I'm not being unreasonable . . . OK, OK, I'll do it . . . Yeah, yeah, yeah. Tickets at the front desk. Gerry at one o'clock. Got it . . . No, I don't need to write it down.' Molly paused. She was in a filthy mood. 'I'll see you later.' Molly clunked the phone down.

Micky stood in the doorway. 'Never seen you so grumpy.'

Molly snarled at him: 'Don't want to go back, that's all. The flight's tomorrow. Also, Gerry arrives at Quito airport at one o'clock today. I have to go and pick him up. He's coming back to England with us.'

'I'll go and get him.'

'Don't be stupid, Micky. You don't even know what he looks like.'

Petula came up to Molly and sniffed her. She smelt of burnt sticks. Petula knew Molly really well. This smell meant that she was very, very cross. Petula wondered why. Molly had woken up in such a good mood.

'I'm pleased we're going home,' Micky declared. He pulled his bag out to start packing. 'It will be

8

really nice to see Ojas and Rocky.'

Molly shut her eyes. She felt a bit odd. Everything felt extra irritating. Maybe it was the tea. She usually drank concentrated orange squash. Perhaps the tea had some angry-making spice in it or maybe it was full of caffeine. It should have a warning on the side of the box. Instead of saying 'May cause drowsiness' like some things do, it should say 'May cause anger and irritability'.

Molly glanced about the room and then her eyes fell upon a painting on the wall of flowers in a golden pot. It really was exquisite. At once she felt better. Like fire put out by water, her anger was quelled. And suddenly she felt that these emotions were all new. It was as if she had never felt anger before and never appreciated beauty. All of it seemed new and fresh. She stood up and stretched. As she passed Micky, she patted his shoulder.

'Sorry about that,' she apologized. 'I don't know why I got so annoyed. Sorry.'

'That's OK. It's just I'm not used to you being bad-tempered,' Micky said. 'You're usually so nice.'

Outside on the main street they heard the sound of cheering. Molly went to the balcony and looked over.

The Japanese boy band was leaving in a limousine and fans had gathered to snap their pictures and gawp. Molly watched as bodyguards guided the boys into the car. Then she noticed more bodyguards shepherding a smaller person in with them.

'I thought there were only three boys in the band,'

Molly said to Micky, who had come to peer over the balcony with her.

'There are. That tiny man's their manager. He's called Mr Proila – and he's mean. He controls them. You think Lucy and Primo are bad, but they're nothing compared to him.'

Molly shrugged and glanced at her watch.

'Petula, come on. It's time to collect Gerry from the airport.'

Chapter Two

Petula sniffed at Molly. The nasty smell had gone. Seeing her open the door, she dropped the stone that she'd been sucking and trotted after Molly along the hotel's carpeted corridor. At the top of the stairs they paused. Molly gave Petula a competitive look and then, suddenly, they both raced down.

'Next time I'll win,' Molly laughed, arriving at the bottom of the stairs. Petula wagged her curly tail.

Molly half walked, half skidded across the white marble lobby and through the rotating hotel door, and she and Petula stepped out into the Ecuadorian sunshine.

'Hat for dog? I make she small one.' A woman in a trilby was selling hats outside the hotel. Molly had already bought six of them.

Molly smiled. She felt sorry for this woman, who worked such long hours and sold her hats for so little.

'All right. You can post it to me when it's done. Like the others. Thank you.'

'Thank you. You good girl,' the woman said with a wink. 'See you later.'

Molly and Petula walked to a queue of black and white taxis. Molly waved at the driver of the first cab and she opened its door.

Soon they were driving up the steep, narrow streets that climbed out of Quito town to the suburbs beyond. Little houses and small apartment blocks clung to the slopes, patchworking the mountainsides with brightly painted brick walls and corrugated roofs.

Molly looked at her watch. A little bored, she decided to entertain herself by dipping into Petula's mind to see what she was thinking. She loved reading Petula's mind for it made her feel closer to her. Focusing, she asked, 'What are you thinking?'

Instantaneously a bubble popped up over her pug's head. Inside the bubble were pictures of the fields outside the window, and of Petula running through them, and then of the fields back home. Molly let the bubble pop. She gave Petula a big cuddle.

'So you're feeling homesick, are you, Petula? Yes, it is very selfish of me to think of staying out here. We'll go back to England soon.'

When they arrived at the airport, Molly discovered that the plane was late. To fill the time, and because she liked to help people, she decided to use her skills to fix a few things. She hypnotized a fretful baby so that it went to sleep in its pushchair then a spotty teenage girl to stop her worrying about her acne and to eat less greasy food and chocolate. She hypnotized a bad-tempered man to be more charming. Still with time on her hands, Molly made friends with the airport-cafe waitress and helped her clear tables, and then she rounded up trolleys and parked them near the entrance of the airport. Three and a half hours later, she stood leaning against a rail in the arrivals area with Petula on the ground beside her.

'LOS ANGELES WW328 . . . LANDED . . . 15:45', the arrivals board finally read.

Molly and Petula watched as travellers of all shapes and all colours rolled luggage out from the baggage-reclaim area. They popped through like travellers coming off a factory conveyor belt, until at last a tanned eight-year-old boy burst through the swing door.

Gerry was in a white shirt with flowers on it and wore a blue straw hat with a small brim that he kept tapping down as though worried it might come off. His face lit up when he saw Molly.

'MOLLY!' he shouted. He turned to a uniformed air stewardess who was walking alongside him, said something to her and pointed his finger at Molly. The air stewardess nodded. Gerry rushed forward, ducked under the rail, one hand firmly keeping his hat on, and threw his free arm about her waist. Molly hugged him back. They hadn't seen each other for a long time.

'I can't believe it! It really is you, Molly! I can't believe it!' His accent was as Cockney as it had been when he'd lived at the orphanage. Then Gerry spotted Petula. 'Amazin'! Is that Petula?' He bent down and hugged her too. Petula licked his face. Odd, she thought. Gerry had a strong smell of mouse about him.

'Uh-hmm,' coughed the tall stewardess beside him in an official tone. 'So, Gerry, where is your guardian? I have to sign you over to a guardian, you see. I can't let you go until then.'

'This is 'er,' Gerry blurted out.

'Oh no, sorry.' The stewardess laughed. 'The person has to be a grown-up. Young lady, is your mother or your aunt about? She's called Mrs Moon.'

Molly saw what had happened. Gerry had travelled unaccompanied and Lucy Logan must have given Molly's name as the grown-up who was going to meet him when he got off the plane. She knew Molly would be able to handle this problem. A little hypnotism was what was needed, that was all. Molly put her hand under the air hostess's elbow and gently led her away from Gerry. Then she centred herself and looked up at the young woman to concentrate on how she should hypnotize her. The lady was brisk and efficient, tight like a coiled spring but not unkind. Capturing this essence of her, and trying to make herself feel this way too, Molly turned her eyes on.

They throbbed as they drove a hypnotic glare into the woman's brown eyes.

'She's . . . she's . . .' The woman stumbled over her words. 'She's called Mrs, erm, Mrs . . .'

'Mrs Moon?' Molly asked.

'Y-yes.'

Molly felt the fusion feeling – a wave of warm tingling that started in her toes and enveloped her body, making the hairs on the back of her neck stand on end – and she knew the woman was hypnotized.

She kept looking into her eyes as she said, 'I am Mrs Moon. I am the boy's mother. I may not look it, but I am. I'm thirty-five years old.'

The woman nodded dumbly and smiled like a baby who's just been given an ice cream.

'Good,' she replied. 'Sign here then, please, and you can take him away.'

'In half an hour you will no longer be hypnotized by me,' Molly whispered. 'You will remember that you handed Gerry Oakly over to a woman who looks like I will when I'm grown up.' Molly paused. If she could, she always liked to leave people with something good after she'd hypnotized them. 'From now on, you will be very happy. You will dance . . . a lot. Got that?'

The woman nodded. 'Goodbye,' she said. Smiling blissfully, she turned and began walking away across the terrazzo airport floor. Halfway across she stopped. She did a little balletic twirl, which was applauded by an old man with a walking stick. Gerry let Petula go just in time to see the air hostess pirouette through a queue of teenage students and disappear.

'She's cheered up!' he remarked. 'She wasn't all dancey like that on the plane!'

'Maybe she's not allowed to dance on the plane,' said Molly.

Gerry shrugged. Then a naughty look crossed his face. He glanced about. Carefully he took off his blue straw hat.

'Look,' he said. 'I made a secret compartment in it.'

Molly looked into the crown of the hat, where a black cloth lining had been sewn in. All of a sudden it moved.

'Oh! Is it Titch the second?'

'The Third,' Gerry said sadly. 'A cat got number two.'

Petula winced when she heard the word 'cat'. She hated cats. But the smell of mouse coming from the hat distracted her. She lifted her nose to get a better whiff.

'Did you travel all the way from LA with him in there?'

'Yeah.' Gerry undid a Velcro join in the lining and a brown mouse stuck his nose out.

'But didn't they catch you at the X-ray machine?'

'No. I just walked through with my hat on and they were so busy they didn't even notice.'

'What about on the plane?' Molly asked, amazed.

'Oh, Titch enjoyed it. I gave 'im some exercise in the basin of the aeroplane toilet. An' he slept. An' I gave 'im some cheese. That stewardess was in a dream or somethin'. Loads of times my 'at was bobbin' about like crazy on my 'ead but she didn't seem to notice.'

'Didn't he, um, wee on you?' Molly asked.

Gerry scratched his hair. 'Erm, a bit, I s'pose. But Titch's pee don't really smell.'

Petula cocked her head and sniffed the air. Molly wrinkled her nose too.

'Hmm.' She laughed. 'That's a matter of opinion. Maybe you should have made him a kind of mouse nappy.'

Gerry grinned. 'Maybe next time.'

Molly hugged Gerry around his shoulders. He was a lot shorter than her, which wasn't surprising as he was much younger. She was really glad to see him.

In the cab on the way back to the hotel Gerry told Molly about his new life in America. The large mansion that belonged to Primo Cell, Molly's father, was a far cry from Hardwick House, the dump where he and Molly and Rocky and the other orphans had grown up. It had indoor and outdoor pools, a games room with ping-pong and tenpin bowling, and each one of the nine adopted orphans had their own bedroom.

Mrs Trinklebury, the woman who had once worked as a cleaner in the orphanage, was now in charge. She had enrolled the children into a progressive school where they grew vegetables, cooked, did lots of art and music, and where English, history, geography, science and even maths lessons were, Gerry said, fun.

'Fun?' Molly asked incredulously.

'Yeah,' Gerry said keenly. 'English is just books, and the teacher reads 'em to us too. It's just like story time all the time. And maths isn't like maths, because the teacher is so funny. He's got a parrot that talks all the sums! An' history is like scary stories about what's 'appened in the

17

world so far, and the way the teacher tells it you don't wanna leave the class, the stories are that good. An' the geography lesson makes you want to get on an aeroplane and see all the countries. An' we do a class called natural world. We learned all about endangered species.' Gerry gazed out of the window, his eyes turning misty. 'It's really sad what's 'appening to the rainforests,' he said as they passed a copse of trees. 'And 'orrible about the seas an' the whales.'

Molly stroked Petula.

'People are pollutin' the seas, fishin' all the fish, huntin' and killin' the whales, even though they're endangered. One day there might not be fish left. Some grown-ups are sick.' Gerry opened the window and then wound it up again, as though to clear his mind.

'Music lessons are really cool. We made our own instruments out of oil drums and saws and glass bottles. An' we formed a band and played our crazy instruments and the teacher was the conductor.'

Molly was impressed. Perhaps she could hypnotize the tutor waiting for them back home to be like these teachers.

'I'm learnin' the mouth organ, and –' Gerry's hand dived into his pocket – 'this one is for you.' He passed Molly a silver harmonica. 'Bought it with me own pocket money.'

'HARMONY' was etched across the top side of the instrument.

'Oh, thank you so much,' Molly said gratefully. 'I really like it.' She gave it a blow and they both laughed at the noise she produced.

'If you practise, you'll get better,' said Gerry. 'I was bad too when I started.' He then took another mouth organ out of his pocket and gave Molly a demonstration. 'Oh . . . yeeeeeah,' he said when he finished.

Molly laughed. 'Brilliant!' she said.

'An' I wrote this one about the whales. I did it for my endangered-species project.'

This time Gerry played a mournful tune. In between chords he made a strange, guttural noise with a high-pitched call mixed into it. That was his impersonation of a whale, Molly realized. Though it was actually quite funny, she didn't laugh. Gerry was obviously deadly serious and she didn't want to hurt his feelings. Little did she know that in a matter of days she would be far less considerate, and Gerry would be wondering where the kind Molly had gone.

Chapter Three

Gerry, chatty as a chaffinch, filled Molly in about his life in America, making her laugh with his funny impersonations. She was very glad that she'd gone to the airport to meet him. Gerry did stink a bit of mouse pee, but it was really terrific to see him again.

Back in central Quito the cab stopped short of the hotel. The alley to the square was so crowded with people the driver couldn't get any closer. Hordes of fans, who had flocked into the city to see the Japanese boy band play that evening, were gathered outside the hotel. Molly paid the cab driver, picked up Petula and, with Gerry holding on tightly to his hat and his bag, they tried to push through.

'When you was in New York in that Broadway show, was it like this?' Gerry asked as they squeezed through the crowd.

Molly wondered whether to tell Gerry that she had become a star on Broadway by hypnotizing an agent and a producer to get a part in a show, and then by hypnotizing everyone including the audience to think that she was the most talented performer ever. She was still ashamed when she remembered how she had become a star by conning people. Gerry would be shocked by how selfish she'd been. She would never use her hypnotism in such a way again, she thought. She decided not to explain what had really happened. Instead she laughed.

'Oh, I wasn't as big as these guys. They're huge!'

'You were good though, Molly. All the papers said so.'

'You know what they say – don't believe everything you read in the papers.' Molly smiled.

Finally Molly and Gerry made it to the hotel lift. A flustered bellboy stopped them briefly, then recognized Molly and Petula, and pressed the lift button for them.

'Oh, puppy,' he gasped to Petula, stroking her head. 'Zis is crazeey.'

Inside the suite, Micky was lying on his bed reading. Petula bounded in and jumped up to greet him.

'You've been ages!' Micky said, sitting up and smiling at Gerry. 'You must be Gerry. I'm Micky.' He reached out to shake hands. Seeing a mouse in Gerry's hand, he faltered.

'This is Titch. And, yeah, I'm Gerry. Hello.'

'Gerry's going to have a shower,' Molly said, surreptitiously pointing to Gerry's hair and holding her nose, 'because Titch has had a long journey – on Gerry's head.'

21

'After that we can go and see the Japanese boys,' Micky suggested. 'They've given us VIP tickets for their concert tonight. Want to go?'

'You bet,' said Gerry. 'But with all them fans downstairs,' he went on, 'they'll probably have to leave from a secret door.'

'You're right.' Micky smiled again at Gerry. 'The passes they've given us get us into the stadium through a special door *and* we get to go to the party afterwards. But you'll have to leave Titch here with Petula. OK? And –' he looked at his watch – 'we leave soon.'

While Gerry was in the shower, Molly changed her top for a black and white stripy long-sleeved one. Gerry came out of his room in jeans and a T-shirt with a whale on it. He made a nest for Titch in a box with holes in its lid, and Molly left Petula a bowl of water.

After a quick snack of tortilla chips and guacamole, they were ready.

Before they left the room, Molly's eyes darted around to see whether she'd left anything behind. On the table she saw the black velvet pouch with the gold coin in it. For some reason she didn't want to leave it behind. She picked it up, left the room and closed the door behind her.

Quito Stadium stood on the outskirts of the city like some sort of giant metal spaceship. The cab Molly, Micky and Gerry were in drove through a special guests' gate and soon it pulled up at the performers' entrance to the building. Micky knocked on the door and a serious-faced man opened it. He looked at their passes. Then he nodded and accompanied them along a series of grey passages and up several flights of stairs into the heart of the building. As they followed him, the noise of an audience somewhere beyond thumped through the walls. The man turned the handle of a white door. 'Kids, after the show, follow that passage upstairs,' he said, pointing behind them. 'That's where the party is. Enjoy the gig!'

He opened the door and Molly, Micky and Gerry were hit by a wall of sound. They walked on to a private balcony that had a perfect view of the stage. The auditorium below and about them was heaving.

'What's the band called?' Molly shouted to Micky.

'Zagger.'

The friends peered down.

'Glad we're not down there,' said Micky, looking at the fans at the very front of the crowd in the mosh pit below.

'Yeah, you'd get mashed up like a stick on a stormy night,' Gerry observed.

Micky laughed. 'Squashed like a beetle in a mud flood!'

Molly gave him a hug. 'It's really nice to see you, Gerry,' she said. 'I've missed you.'

A deep voice came over the loudspeakers: '*Señoras y señores!* Ladies and gentlemen. *El momento que ustedes esperan* . . . The moment you are waiting for . . . *De la bienvenida por favor . . . ZAGGER!*'

The audience erupted. And the stage came to life. A silver drum kit with a halo of lights above it rose in the very centre. Banks of keyboards, glowing with yellow light, emerged to the left, and an electric guitar picked out in blue neon appeared on the right. More white light revealed a cloud of snowy curtains at the back of the stage. These parted and three boys, each one dressed in a sharp silver spacesuit, stepped out towards the audience.

The boys looked amazing. Their hair jutted up, cutting the air so that they looked like strange bird-boys. The tallest one's Mohican was orange, the middle boy's was red and the smallest's was green. Their silver suits had peaked shoulder pieces that gave the impression that they might suddenly spread wings and fly. Molly looked at Gerry's face and smiled. He was enraptured.

The smallest band member, a boy who was very solidly built, leaped up on to the drum rostrum and sat down. Picking up two black sticks, he began to play. Fierce and precise, he beat out a rhythm that soon had the audience whooping and cheering.

While the drummer drummed, the tallest boy went to the keyboards and the other one to the guitar, which had a microphone stand near it. The drumming suddenly stopped.

'Hellooooo, Quito!' the tallest boy shouted into his microphone in a strong Japanese accent. 'How ya doin'? You ready for some show?'

The audience whistled and cheered.

'OK. You ready, Chokichi?'

The boy on the electric guitar gave his brother a thumbs-up.

24

'You ready, Toka?'

The drummer nodded and leaned towards his microphone. 'You too, Hiroyuki?'

'You bet!' Hiroyuki replied. 'Here we go . . . A one, a two, a one two three four.'

And then the music started. It was mad. It was amazing. And mostly it was in Japanese. But this didn't bother the audience, because they loved watching the band perform. The boys played fast tunes that had the whole audience jumping and slow songs that the crowd swayed and waved their hands to. After four songs they went offstage and minutes later came back on in glittering costumes. A screen behind them lit up with pictures of rare animals, and they performed some more. For the show's finale they changed into karate outfits. Chokichi did a fast karate-style dance that ended with a flying leap and a somersault kick into a papier mâché tiger that burst, releasing confetti. At the same time confetti exploded over the audience and fell like snow.

At the end, the band came back onstage (this time in black spacesuits) to rapturous applause. When they fianlly left the stage, the lights dimmed and the sweaty but satisfied crowd started to leave.

'Let's go to the party!' said Micky.

Chapter Four

Molly, Micky and Gerry made their way to the staircase that led to the VIP party room. Other people jostled their way past them. Ahead, the noise of the after party grew louder.

A bouncer stood at the door, burly and unmoving.

'Name?' he asked, referring to a list.

Micky gave their names and they were through. Beyond was a large room with a dark blue ceiling dotted with lights like stars. The walls were covered with hundreds of tiny soft lights shaped like ivy leaves and the room was full of expectant people.

Molly glanced about. The band hadn't arrived yet. She, Micky and Gerry crossed the room to a seating area with a door leading off it. Before anyone knew what Gerry was up to, he walked up to this door and pushed it open.

'I don't think you're supposed to go in th . . .' started

Micky. But Gerry had already slipped through.

Molly looked around. No one had taken any notice. She went through too. Nervously, Micky followed.

Beyond the door a passage opened into a hexagonal space with more doors set in four of the walls. A big round sofa strewn with cushions and sheepskins sat in the middle like a huge, hairy slug.

'Why did you come in here?' Molly whispered to Gerry.

Gerry shrugged, but before he could reply, a booming voice made them all jump. 'Fifth rate! That's what it was!'

'Sounds like a Russian accent,' Micky mouthed to Molly.

The voice continued. 'You, Hiroyuki – Miss Sny tells me you sang flat ten times. *And* you were slow to come on in three numbers. Miss Sny noted every mistake down, so don't think you can get away with it.'

Silently Molly, Micky and Gerry moved closer to a door that was slightly ajar.

In the room beyond, Molly could see part of a mirror and a chair on wheels, on which was perched a nervous-looking Japanese woman in a black suit. She was holding a pen and pad. Was this the Miss Sny the cross Russian-sounding man had referred to?

'And,' the thickly accented voice went on, 'your footwork was lousy. I may be deaf, but I'm not blind. That break-dancing you did – well, you shouldn't have bothered! And you, Chokichi . . .' Molly saw a little hairy hand pointing. 'Your energy was dismal. Your karate dance was a disaster – even worse than Hiroyuki's efforts.

And, Toka . . .' Molly saw a small man in profile. She realized that he was the one she had seen getting into the limo with the band earlier. The one Micky had said was the band's manager. '. . . Your drumsticks were as weak as jelly chopsticks in your hands. Pathetic! No strength! The others could have performed without you.'

The man stepped forward so that now Molly got a good look at him. He was still shouting. His fat face and bulbous nose were pitted and scarred, his eyes small and sunken as a pig's and his rubbery mouth, fringed by a bristly black moustache, looked mean. The hair on his head was short as a mole's. He held a cigar between his teeth and on his feet he wore white shoes with a substantial heel, presumably in an attempt to give himself extra height.

Molly decided to take a look at what was going on in his head. Quickly she summoned a thought bubble to appear above him. Oddly, inside it was an image of a boot pressing down on the head of each of the Japanese boys. Molly let the bubble pop.

'I'm telling you,' the bullying manager went on, 'if it goes on like this, you're all finished. I'll find another band. Then you will all be has-beens, yesterdayers – washed up, with no one interested in anything you do.'

With that, the man turned to the door. Molly, Micky and Gerry dived for the sofa and covered themselves with sheepskins and cushions.

'Oh, and you are to stay in this room. You're banned from the party.'

Fiery with fury, he steamed out. Molly poked her head from under her sheepskin rug to see him go. Hot on his heels was his efficient-looking assistant. They walked away, Miss Sny trying to keep up so that he could read her lips.

'But, Mr Proila, their CD is very good . . . really it is, Mr Proila,' she said. 'And Chokichi played the new number very—'

All of a sudden there was a squeal from Miss Sny. Mr Proila had punched her arm.

'Shut it, Sny, or I'll shut it for you.' The door to the party room opened, producing a wave of noise. Mr Proila marched through, slamming the door in Miss Sny's face.

'*Baka!*' she muttered. Rubbing her arm, she took a moment to pull herself together and then followed her boss.

Molly threw the rug off herself.

'Coast clear,' she whispered, and Micky and Gerry emerged too.

'He's a nasty piece of work,' Micky said quietly. 'Let's go and see the boys.' He knocked on the door and entered.

Chapter Five

The boy band were sitting together on the sofa in their dressing room with stunned looks on their faces. The biggest one, whose expression was the most forlorn, was fumbling distractedly with a piece of paper, folding it and tapping it.

Molly, Micky and Gerry edged into the room.

'Hi, guys. Great show,' said Micky gently.

'You were brilliant,' added Molly.

'The best band I've ever seen live,' enthused Gerry, pushing from behind. 'Well, actually the first band I've ever seen live, but, still, you were A-MAZING.'

'Glad someone thought so.' Hiroyuki, the boy with the paper in his hands, smiled. 'My keyboards weren't good. Apparently we were sucking.'

'You were sucking what?' asked Gerry.

'He means we sucked,' explained Chokichi. 'His

English is sometimes a bit wrong.'

'You didn't,' said Molly, stepping closer. 'You were really good. That man doesn't know what he's talking about.'

'Is he your dad?' asked Gerry.

'No,' Chokichi replied, half laughing. 'He's our manager.'

'He's putting you down,' said Molly, 'so that you think you're so bad that no one else will ever manage you. It's because you're so *good* that he's doing it. He doesn't want you to leave him.'

'You think so?' said Toka, the small muscly one. 'Because he real mean just then. I don't like performing anyway. An' his meanness make me want to kit.'

'To kit?'

'He means quit,' explained Chokichi.

'Well, he's wrong,' Molly assured Toka.

The band boys looked at each other and perked up a little.

'Thanks for coming, Micky,' said Hiroyuki. 'And this your sister Molly?'

Micky nodded. 'And this is Gerry.'

'Hi, guys,' said Hiroyuki.

Chokichi and Toka got up and shook hands formally. 'Hi,' they echoed.

To break the embarrassed silence, Hiroyuki passed Gerry the paper he was holding. It was cleverly folded into the shape of a small elephant. 'Here, for you. It *baku*. Special Japanese spirit creature. It have trunk and tusk of

31

elephant but feet of tiger. It eat bad dreams.'

'Wow!' said Gerry. 'Thanks. Does it work?'

'Work for me.'

'That lady said the word *baku* after your manager thumped her.'

Hiroyuki laughed. 'No, she said, "*baka*" – means "idiot". Poor Miss Sny. Mr Proila is so mean to her.'

'You're really good at folding paper!' Gerry said.

'It's "origami",' said Chokichi. 'That one nothing. Look there.' He pointed to Hiroyuki's dressing table where an array of little animals stood. The children went over to admire them.

'Wow, they must have taken ages,' Micky said admiringly.

'Not so long,' Hiroyuki laughed. 'They magic animals – called "*henge*". I make before show tonight. Calm my nerves.'

'I'll order up some drinks and more snacks,' said Toka, slapping his knees. He went over to the phone.

'Nice room you've got here,' said Molly, walking across to one of the pinball machines. She felt in her pocket for some change. Her fingers closed around the gold coin in its black pouch and she couldn't resist pulling it out to have a look at it.

'Oh, you don't need money for them.' Chokichi laughed, joining Molly. 'You just press that button.' His eyes fell upon the gold coin. 'Wow! What's that?'

Molly showed the coin to him, tossing it lightly in the air so that he saw both its sides but not letting him touch it. The coin landed in her hand, musical note up. A very strong feeling had suddenly gripped her. She really, really did not want Chokichi to touch her coin.

'It's nothing,' she said nonchalantly.

'Looks like it's for people who love music, with that note etched on it,' said Chokichi.

'I suppose it is.' Molly put the coin in its black pouch and quickly slipped it back into her pocket. 'Is this the thing to pull?' she asked, changing the subject and pointing to a knob on the pinball machine. She pulled back the starter mechanism and let it go.

A small steel ball ricocheted around the obstacle course inside the machine. Gerry came over to see what they were doing.

Molly stood aside to let him take over the paddles. 'So how long are you here?' she asked Hiroyuki.

'Till midday tomorrow. Then long flight back to Japan. And you?'

'Not sure yet.' There was a pause. 'How come that horrible man is your manager?' Molly asked.

Hiroyuki sighed. 'Mr Proila discover us when we young. Our parents are poor.' Absent-mindedly he picked up a piece of brown paper and began folding it. Molly watched his fingers move dextrously. 'They signed contract with him. We sing and our parents and our family have better life because of contract. Mr Proila manage us; make sure we rehearse, book our tours, get our CDs in shops. He deaf, you know. He mean. But he also very rich and powerful. Very successful.' He paused as he finished the little origami sculpture. 'This is *Shishi* lion. See open mouth? That to scare off evil spirits.' At an incredible speed he made another. 'This his twin. This *Shishi* have closed mouth to keep good spirits safe.' He put the lions together. 'So, what you doing here?'

Molly wondered whether to tell Hiroyuki about what they'd been doing in Ecuador. 'We're on a break, a mini-holiday.' Molly sipped some more of her tea.

'So now you go home?'

'Yes, but I *really* don't want to!' Molly confided.

'Come to Japan with us! Plenty of room on plane.'

Molly nodded. 'Wow. Wish I could. But I can't.'

The rest of the evening was spent in the adjoining games room. There was a mini shooting gallery, an indoor boules pitch and a roulette wheel. The hours rolled by. Fuelled with sugary fizzy drinks and snacks, they played past midnight.

'I can hardly keep my eyes open, and no wonder – it's one o'clock,' said Molly, looking at her watch.

Micky yawned. 'I suppose we should go.'

'That was the best fun,' said Gerry, giving Toka a friendly slap on the shoulder. 'I could play all night.'

'Have a good trip home,' Chokichi said as everyone gathered their things.

'And remember,' said Hiroyuki at the door, 'you're welcome to join us and come to Japan. We have private plane, so it really easy. All you need do –' he handed Molly a piece of paper with a name and number on it – 'is call this number. Speak to Miss Yjuko. She air hostess of plane. She tell you where plane leaves and what time.'

Molly smiled. 'I think we'll more likely see you when you come on tour to London. But thanks, Hiroyuki. A nice idea.'

Back at the hotel, Micky and Gerry went to bed.

'Do you think *baku* really eats the bad dreams?' Molly heard Gerry asking as the door shut.

Molly stayed up for a bit. She walked out on to the balcony and sat down. She put the black pouch on the table and absent-mindedly pulled out her gold coin. She wound it between her fingers. Then she looked at the card Hiroyuki had given her. It would be really fun to go to Tokyo in a private jet with him and his brothers. Instead she had to go back to England, to school.

She looked out across the city square. The old buildings of Quito stood before her, their facades lit up. They looked like an audience waiting for something.

In her pocket was the mouth organ that Gerry had given her. Molly pulled it out and put it to her lips. And she blew. She was surprised to find that the sound she made wasn't bad at all. Amazingly she found that she was playing a tune that she didn't even think she knew.

Below, a tramp in the square pulled his blanket around himself and listened to Molly's music. He took his woolly hat off to hear better. When the music finished, he clapped. 'Bravo! Bravo!' he shouted enthusiastically.

Molly stood up and nodded to him and waved. The

music she'd played had been remarkable, she thought, for a beginner. Then she noticed an even older man in a tweed suit who had appeared suddenly beside the tramp on the bench. She wondered who he was and where he'd come from. His clothes were strange for the city he was in, and old-fashioned too. Not wanting an audience, Molly sat back down out of sight.

She rolled her golden coin between her thumb and forefinger. The musical note engraved on it stared back at her. Molly had the peculiar sensation that the coin was actually trying to speak to her, telling her what to do. She thought again about Japan, all the time looking at the golden coin.

'That's decided then,' she said. 'I am going to Japan.'

Chapter Six

Molly woke early and reached immediately for the black pouch she'd tucked beneath her pillow before falling asleep.

Her head felt clearer than the night before. Disobeying her parents and going to Japan against their wishes didn't seem like a big deal now. She got out of bed and began packing.

Once her small case was packed and by the door, she collected up her brother's and Gerry's scattered things and packed for them too. If they wouldn't come with her, they'd be going back to England. Either way, they'd be checking out of the hotel. She knew Japan wouldn't be as much fun without them. She hoped she'd be able to persuade them to come. She found everyone's passports.

As soon as she was dressed, she stuffed the black pouch with her special coin into her pocket and looked at the piece of paper Hiroyuki had given her. She picked up the phone and dialled.

'Oh, hello. Is that Miss Yjuko?' she asked when the phone was answered. 'Great. Well, my name's Molly – Molly Moon. Hiroyuki gave me your number. He said to call if I wanted to come on the flight to Tokyo today.

'Thanks. There will probably be three of us, and a dog,' Molly explained, after Miss Yjuko had given her instructions.

Feeling excited and satisfied, Molly hung up the phone and bent down to do up her shoes. A shadow crossed her feet. She looked up. Micky was glowering at her. His hair was ruffled from sleep and his eyes were puffy.

'What are you doing booking us all on a flight to Tokyo?' he growled. 'We're going back home tonight, Molly.'

'I'm not,' Molly answered, crossing her arms defiantly. 'You don't have to come, but I don't have to go with you either.'

'You can't just go off when Lucy and Primo want you home,' said Micky. 'They're our parents. Remember what it was like in the orphanage? You said you used to wish for parents all the time. Now you've got them, you're acting as if you don't want them.'

Molly frowned. Why couldn't Micky be reasonable about this?

'Micky, don't make a mountain out of an ant hill.'

'But Rocky really wants to see you.'

Rocky's face flashed across Molly's mind. 'Well, he's

38

always wanted to go to Japan. He can come too.'

She took out her gold coin. Micky was being really irritating about this. She glared at him.

'What's the matter with you? I never knew you were so . . . so selfish and pig-headed.' Exasperated, Micky stomped into the bathroom and shut the door.

'What's up with him?' Gerry asked in bewilderment, coming into the room with Titch in his hands.

Molly put away her coin and pulled out her mouth organ.

'He's a bit –' she blew a sharply crescendoing of notes – 'uptight.'

'Wow, you're pretty good at that thing,' Gerry said, forgetting for a moment about Micky. 'It's you who's going to have to give me lessons! Anyway, what was Micky upset about?'

'It's like this. Either we go back to England or we don't. Primo and Lucy aren't even going to *be* at Briersville because they're going on holiday. We will have to do lessons and chores. Primo and Lucy are just like an orphanage master and mistress, Gerry. The only difference between Briersville Park and Hardwick House is that the house is posh.'

'Really?' Gerry looked horrified.

'Or,' Molly continued, 'we get on the plane today and go to Tokyo and have an amazing time. Japan is surrounded by sea. Maybe we can even do something about those horrible people who are killing whales. I mean, you'd like to do that, wouldn't you?'

Micky came out of the bathroom, dressed. Petula, who had just woken up, followed him into the sitting room. Molly stood up. She fanned their passports out like a hand of winning cards.

'So, are you coming, Micky?' she asked.

Micky shook his head.

'Well, Gerry's coming with me. And Petula.'

'And Titch,' Gerry added.

Petula looked up quizzically, wondering why Micky and Molly were angry with each other. They'd never had a row before. Micky's anger smelt sad, with salt in it. Molly's was less fierce but smelt worse, acrid and sour. There was that sharp lemony smell again. Petula didn't like it one bit.

'You should come, Micky. It's gonna be fun!' Gerry insisted, friendly as a puppy.

'I know,' said Micky sadly. 'But, Gerry, we've got a home, and we were actually on our way back to it. That's where I want to be, with our family.'

Molly went to the door, unhooked her black jacket and gave a short whistle. Petula felt torn. She loved Molly but didn't want to leave Micky. But, more than this torn feeling, she was worried. Molly was normally a very kind person, not prone to nastiness at all. Yet here she was being horrible to her brother and she didn't seem to care that he was upset. To Petula, Molly's anger wasn't the humdrum temporary irritation that can fly between brothers and sisters. It was something more serious and dark. What's more, this strange behaviour had started so suddenly and so recently. Petula was really concerned. Her instinct told her that she must go with Molly to watch over her.

Petula rubbed her head against Micky's legs to say goodbye and to apologize. Then she followed Molly and Gerry down the corridor.

When the lift arrived, Molly let Gerry and Petula get in first.

'Go and get into a cab. I'll meet you outside in a minute. I've forgotten something.'

When she went back into the room, Micky was standing by the bed. His expression brightened when he saw her. 'Changed your mind?'

'I'm sorry, I have to do this,' Molly said. She raised her eyes to Micky's. Her pupils were already charged with high-voltage hypnotic glare. The instant his eyes met hers, Micky was caught. He fell under Molly's spell immediately. The fusion feeling rose up from her feet and flooded through her body. Micky was well and truly hypnotized. He stood in front of her, his mouth open and his eyes glazed.

'Micky,' Molly began, 'you are now under my power. When you wake up from this trance, you won't remember the Japanese boy band at all. You won't remember spending time with them, or seeing their concert. You won't remember them when you think of Japan. In fact, you won't think of Japan much at all. You will forget Mr Proila and Miss Sny and you will forget we argued. You will tell Primo and Lucy that Gerry and I are travelling around South America. You will be happy about all of this, and in a minute when I click my fingers and you wake up you won't remember I hypnotized you.' Molly paused. She had to make sure that her hypnotism couldn't be tampered with. Lucy or Primo were accomplished hypnotists themselves. So she finished, 'And I lock these instructions in with the password "golden coin".'

With that, Molly clicked her fingers and felt immediately for her own gold coin. Micky stood still, blinking rapidly for a few seconds. Then, 'Have a great trip, Molly!' he gushed. 'Send me a postcard.'

Molly ruffled his hair. 'Will do. Bye, Micky.'

With that, she left him again, now with a spring in her step.

Chapter Seven

The taxi drove Molly, Gerry, Petula and Titch straight on to the private terminal tarmac at Quito airport and stopped fifty metres from where the jets were parked. The small luxurious planes stood, sleekly and silently, like beautiful metal sky creatures resting in the morning sun.

Molly saw the Japanese boys beside one plane, talking to the pilot. She smiled. She felt a bit bad about having hypnotized Micky but she didn't regret it. If he told Primo and Lucy where she and Gerry really were, they would send Forest out to Japan to get them. No way was she going back until she felt like it.

She and Gerry got out of the car. Gerry tucked Titch into his hat and put his hat on. With Petula following them, they made their way across the yellow-striped tarmac.

'Wow! Nice plane!' said Gerry. 'Is it yours?'

'For today,' said Toka. 'It's hired. Let's get on. Mr Proila is in the front part with Miss Sny. We're in the back. Mr Proila doesn't want to see us or you.'

'He's usually like that,' said Chokichi.

'Really?' said Gerry, following Toka up steps at the rear of the plane.

'Yes. Unless he wants company,' said Chokichi. 'Doesn't really like us much. Loves the money we make him though.'

'That's for sure.' Toka laughed.

'He sounds mean,' Gerry commented. His hat tipped slightly as he spoke, as Titch made himself comfortable, but nobody noticed.

'Did Micky decide not to come?' Hiroyuki asked Molly as they boarded.

'Yes. He's homesick.'

A friendly air hostess nodded to Molly. 'I am Miss Yjuko,' she said. 'I spoke to you this morning. Welcome on board.'

Molly shook her hand. 'Hello, nice to meet you.' She knew that any second this woman would need to see proof of their parents' permission for Gerry and her to be on the plane. Molly needed to sort the situation out urgently. 'Erm, excuse me, Miss Yjuko, before we do passports and stuff, could I have a glass of water, please?'

Miss Yjuko nodded and moved towards the galley. Molly followed her and switched on her eyes. When Miss Yjuko turned, holding out the glass, Molly had her

44

captive. 'You are under my power,' she told her quietly and quickly. She glanced at the others to check no one was watching. 'You now think that you met Gerry's and my guardians at the airport and that they signed papers, but that you left the papers behind.'

Miss Yjuko nodded. 'Yes, I left the file in the airport terminal with my colleague,' she agreed dumbly.

'And you think you have seen our passports,' Molly hurriedly added.

The woman nodded again.

'When we leave the plane,' Molly went on, 'you will have forgotten that we were ever on board. Also you will destroy any records of us that you have. You will not mention to the captain or his co-pilot or to anyone at the airport that we are on board. It must be as if we are not on board. Is that clear?'

'Of – course – miss, whatever – you – say.'

A small part of Molly felt guilty. This part of her knew that Primo and Lucy would worry about where she was. But another part of her felt that it really was their fault that she'd had to do this. They should have given her more freedom. They'd made her rebel, her logic argued. With her hand on the gold coin in its pouch in her pocket, she went and sat with the others.

The plane taxied up the runway and then took off, cutting up through the air.

'This is one of highest airports in world! It is two thousand eight hundred metres above sea level!' Hiroyuki pointed out. Below, Molly watched the buildings, mountains and the green valleys drop away.

'That way good,' Toka said as they climbed higher and higher. He gestured to the left of the plane. 'Pacific Ocean. If you keep going, you get to Galapagos Islands.'

'Oh, I've heard of them,' Gerry shouted eagerly over the roar of the climbing jet engines. 'One of the only places in the world where humans haven't killed all the wild animals.'

'Yeah, it's cool,' Toka said. 'Lots of islands. I want to go there one day and swim with seals. I love animals!'

Gerry laughed. 'So do I! And I hate people killing animals, especially whales.'

'Same here!'

'Do you like mice?'

'Oh yeah,' Toka replied. 'Got six back home.'

'Why didn't you bring them with you?' Gerry took off his hat and began to undo the Velcro of Titch's compartment.

Petula trotted over to join them at the back of the aircraft. The plane had levelled out now and Molly, Gerry and the band boys had started watching a movie. Molly had taken off her black jacket and hung it over the back of her chair. Petula edged her nose close to it.

The golden coin was in the pocket, Petula knew. She could smell it, but – more than this – she could somehow feel it too. It had a pull – a magnetism, she realized. It drew Petula towards it. Something else was happening as well. It was as if Petula could hear the coin *calling* to her with a mesmerizing alluring tune.

Petula's nose went closer and closer to the pocket. Suddenly Molly's hand snatched her jacket away.

'Mine!' she hissed. Her green eyes were almost fiery. Molly had never looked at Petula this way before – ever.

Petula shrank back apologetically, but also very scared. Molly wasn't herself, and Petula had a suspicion that her strange behaviour had something to do with the coin.

Chapter Eight

The flight was eighteen hours long. Although they had left in the morning, it was after lunch the next day when they arrived in Tokyo, due to the time difference. Gerry was the most excited of all of them as the plane approached Narita airport. He tapped the window and bobbed up and down in his seat.

'Look!' he cried. 'Look at the skyscrapers! There's so much glass! Tokyo looks like a space-age city.'

The plane touched down. It taxied to the private-jet hangars. Molly put on her jacket. She was sorry she'd snapped at Petula and so she patted her head.

She looked out of the jet's window. Hordes of Zagger fans were gathered behind the wire fences of the airport.

Miss Sny came through from the front.

'Boys,' she said, pointing to Hiroyuki, Chokichi and Toka, 'you get off at the front. Your friends get off at the back.' She smiled apologetically at Gerry and Molly. 'S-s-sorry,' she stuttered. 'Mr Proila's orders.'

The boys went with her. Then the rear door of the plane opened and Molly, Petula and Gerry stepped out. To their surprise, the crowd erupted – some screaming, some shouting.

'They're Titch's fans,' Gerry joked as they walked towards the terminal. 'Cor blimey,' he added, watching his new friends signing scores of autographs. 'It's a lot of work bein' famous.'

When they reached the airport building, a line of security men made sure the mass of fans waiting there didn't surge forward. Four big bodyguards stood by the door. Hiroyuki, Chokichi and Toka bowed to them and they bowed more deeply back.

They were ushered quickly through all the airport security. Then, as the sliding exit doors opened, the hubbub of cheering and hysterical calling from the fans outside filled the airport hall.

'Look at her!' Gerry said to Molly, pointing at one of the crowd. 'The way she's screamin', it's like there's a monster behind her tryin' to eat her.'

Molly, Gerry and Petula were bundled towards a stretch limo. Still shocked by the size of the welcome for the boy band, they got inside.

Petula jumped on to Gerry's lap as Hiroyuki, Chokichi and Toka clambered in after them.

As they drove into central Tokyo, Molly sank into the padded seat and thought how lovely the boys' lives were and she drank in Tokyo.

The city was enormous. Everywhere was concrete or metal or glass or mirror or tarmac or stone. Molly could see only a few trees.

'What tiny houses!' Molly remarked as they passed through a homely neighbourhood.

'Tiny?' Chokichi exclaimed. 'Those are huge for Tokyo houses. You see, Molly, there isn't enough space here. There are so many people who want to live in the city. Those houses are thought of as very big, very expensive. Rich people live in them.'

'So where do poor people live?' asked Gerry, playing with Titch.

'In *really* tiny houses,' Toka replied.

As he opened a bag of rice crackers, Hiroyuki joined in the conversation. 'Japanese people very good living close together.'

'Look, there is Shinto shrine!' Chokichi said, pointing to a pretty little building held up by red wooden pillars. Its grey roof curved up at the edges like tiled wings. 'We go to shrine and make offerings to good *kami* to help us. Priest give us special *ema* – pieces of wood with good luck written on them. We like *ema*.'

Molly gazed out of the window and fingered her gold coin. She hadn't been listening to the boys. She was thinking that if she lived in Japan she would want a huge, beautiful penthouse at the top of a skyscraper with a view of the whole of Tokyo.

The limo swung through the super-modern main

streets of central Tokyo, where banners hung from shops, flapping in the wind. Office workers in business suits, mothers with pushchairs walked the pavements as well as teenagers who were unlike any teenagers Molly had seen before. A lot of them seemed to be dressed like characters from comics or cartoons.

Finally the car pulled up in front of a very smart building with a polished steel front that reflected the cloudy blue sky. Again, fans were standing about and barriers had been put up to control them.

Gerry was appalled. 'What, they're waiting for you 'ere too? Do they never leave you alone?'

Hiroyuki, Chokichi and Toka laughed as they all got out.

Molly looked up. The green building looked like a huge pea pod, its apartments giant peas.

After another frenzy of starry-eyed fans taking photographs, with Molly and Gerry and Petula waiting inside the marble lobby of the building, the band boys came in. They all stepped into a polished chrome elevator, and up it went to the fourteenth floor.

'Who lives on the floors above?' Molly asked.

'Mr Proila, of course.' Toka grimaced. They stepped out of the lift to a bright landing with a view of the city to their right. 'He's got whole top two floors – sixteenth and seventeenth. And we have fourteenth and fifteenth. There is roof garden on top, but nothing much to see up there at the moment, just some bare cherry trees.'

The black ebony door to the apartment stood ajar. A

round-faced woman in a blue tracksuit waited there with open arms and a smile on her face. Hiroyuki, Chokichi and Toka rushed to hug her.

'Molly, Gerry, meet Miss Shonyo,' said Chokichi. 'She helps us with . . . well, with everything really – especially with food!' He said something in Japanese to Miss Shonyo, who smiled and bowed to Molly and Gerry and Petula.

'Miss Shonyo great cook!' Toka said, patting his big stomach.

Molly and Gerry laughed. Both were thinking that Tokyo looked as if it was going to be a lot of fun.

Chapter Nine

Miss Shonyo held the front door to the apartment open and everyone went in. Just inside was a row of slipper-like shoes that the Japanese brothers started to change into.

'Ah,' said Chokichi. 'Custom of changing shoes is everywhere in Japan. We keep the street dirt outside. We will get you some indoor shoes, but for today just wear socks inside.'

'Sobo?' Hiroyuki called into the apartment. 'Sobo is our grandmother,' he explained to Molly.

The inside of the boys' apartment was lovely. The entrance opened out into a huge modern room with high ceilings and tall elegant windows. A balcony ran along the outside, and a neat spiral staircase at the back of the room led up to a mezzanine platform with doors leading off it.

In the main room the walls were hung with three long tapestries, each a picture of one of the boys surfing. There was a long, orange sofa, and a few giant bright green beanbags that looked like massive squashed peas.

'Make yourself at home,' invited Toka. 'I go sort out where you guys sleep.'

Gerry went with him, and Molly walked over to the windows. Tokyo stretched away for miles. Beyond its urban horizon was the backdrop of a brilliantly blue cloud-specked sky, dotted with helicopters and small aircraft.

As Gerry's excited voice gabbled away upstairs, Molly stood lapping up the city.

'Wonder if Titch will get on with your mice,' Gerry was saying as Toka showed him his bedroom. 'Wow! I've never seen so many posters of sumo wrestlers!'

Petula had followed Gerry upstairs. Now, from the mezzanine, she looked down at Molly. She was a little scared of her now. The way Molly had reacted on the plane had given her a real shock. Petula sighed and watched her lovely Molly as she sat down on the sofa and picked up a book. Petula was convinced that that coin was having a bad effect on her friend.

Something small and hard hit Molly's head. She looked up at the mezzanine expecting to see Gerry there, but the platform was empty. Molly rubbed her head and glanced about her. Something clipped her hard on the cheek and landed on the sofa. It was a dried pea.

She spun around. This time a pea hit her smack on the nose.

The pea seemed to have come from what looked like a miniature shrine that stood up against the wall. Molly went over and peered between the little statues of gods and the decorations of zigzag paper. Was there a hiding place behind the shrine?

Another pea pipped her on the cheek. It had come from a shadowy place under the staircase.

A squeaky rumbling noise came from the darkness. An ancient shrunken woman with a turnip-like head emerged from the gloom. She was in a rickety old wheelchair. She wore a flowered silk kimono, (the traditional dress for Japanese women) and red socks that separated her big toes from the rest. On her lap was a long, apparently hollow, stick. Lifting this to her lips, she dipped her gnarled hand into a bag that was resting on her knees and picked out a pea. This she put into the end of the hollow shooter, and fired again. The pea hit Molly THWACK between the eyes.

'Hey! Hang on a minute!' Molly exclaimed, shocked and affronted. 'What are you doing?'

The old woman laughed and pointed at Molly.

'Hey!' she mimicked, echoing Molly. Like a spook from a nightmare she started to wheel herself forward, her chair squeaking hysterically. Molly stepped backwards but still the woman approached. She wheeled forward until Molly was pinned against the window and the old lady was directly in front of her.

Her skin was thin, creased round her eyes and mouth in well-ironed pleats. Her eyes were long slits and her nose, which she was now wrinkling, was small and flat.

Molly was confused and, she had to admit, a little panicked. Why was this woman being so aggressive? Perhaps she thought Molly was an intruder. Molly assumed the woman was 'Sobo', the grandmother Hiroyuki had called to. She decided to see what was going on in the old lady's mind and so she summoned a thought bubble over her head. For a moment nothing happened. For some reason Molly had to try harder than usual to get a bubble to appear. Eventually one did. And, to Molly's surprise, inside it was an image of herself with devil's horns. The picture was such a shock that Molly lost her focus and the bubble popped.

The old woman spread out her hand, splaying her bent fingers. As if her palm had eyes in it, she moved it in front of Molly's body from left to right and up and down. When she reached Molly's jacket pocket, the old woman pulled back sharply. Her eyes opened in shock, and with a swift jerk of her wheelchair she moved away. Molly reached into her pocket and clutched her coin.

'Aieee!' the old lady exclaimed. With horror on her face, she continued reversing across the room, back to the dark corner where she had been before.

Just then Hiroyuki looked over the platform ledge. 'You want to see room, Molly?' He came down the stairs and saw the old woman's socked feet sticking out from the shadows. 'Oh, and this is Sobo, our grand-mother. She probably too shy to say hello to you. She deaf and can't see well, but she very sweet. She like to hang out under stairs. Small spaces make her feel safe.' The old woman glared from the shadows, silent and wary.

Hiroyuki went towards her and bent into the darkness to give her a kiss. She said something to him in a low rasping voice. Molly felt sure it was something nasty about her. Why had the old woman taken against her? She didn't like it at all. She put her hand into her pocket again and began turning her coin over and over. It was time to change the subject.

'Why don't you live with your parents?' she asked Hiroyuki.

'We want to, but Mr Proila say we have to live with him for band to work. He allow Sobo to come here but not our mother and father. My parents sign contract – so now it cannot change.'

Molly stroked her gold coin. Instead of concentrating on what Hiroyuki was saying, she found herself wondering how much money Zagger made a year.

'One day we will all live together again,' Hiroyuki said. He placed the origami bird that he had made on the table.

Molly didn't hear him. She was totally absorbed in her thoughts. Her eyes fell on a building a couple of blocks away. It had a roller coaster on its roof.

'Wow! I'd love a ride on that! It must be awesome.'

If Molly had been her usual self, she would have been as shocked as Hiroyuki was by her lack of care for his troubles. But she wasn't her usual self. Thanks to the coin, she was growing into something else.

The phone rang. It was Miss Sny.

'What time?' Hiroyuki, who had answered it, asked. 'Fine. Thank you, and can you remind him we've got two guests?' He replaced the receiver. 'Dinner tonight at a restaurant called Mizu,' he explained. 'We have to go whether we like or not. Mr Proila wants to talk to us about big show tomorrow.'

'Tomorrow?'

'Yes, he works us. But we like it . . . or at least Chokichi and I do.'

Petula padded into the room and peered at her mistress warily. The odd smell was back. A thin, sour lemon odour permeated the air about Molly, pungent as steam from a hot sulphurous pool. Petula shrank back.

Chokichi and Toka and Gerry came out on to the mezzanine. Gerry was holding three mice. 'Look, Molly! Titch has got new friends!'

Toka laughed beside him, his own arms filled with well-behaved mice too.

Molly barely smiled back. She wasn't interested in small talk right now. Instead, what made her feel good was that tonight she was going to meet one of the most powerful men in Japan. Since arriving she had become more and more keen on getting a place to live in Tokyo. Mr Proila would be able to help her.

It was a long time since she had used hypnotism to get things for herself. Most people used their skills for their own ends. Hypnotism was her skill. So why shouldn't she use it to get what she wanted?

Chapter Ten

A s they were all jet-lagged, everyone grabbed a few
hours' sleep, and so for the afternoon the
appartment was quiet.

When Molly wandered out of her room later, Chokichi
was already up, practising his karate. Molly watched as
he went through his routine. He moved elegantly back
and forth in front of the large apartment windows, cutting
shapes with his body. When he had finished, he bowed
solemnly to Molly before going upstairs to change.

When everyone was up, the boys' grandmother wheeled
herself into the middle of the sitting room and switched
on her hearing aid so that she could hear her grandsons.
Without acknowledging Molly, she kissed the three boys
and they lavished presents from Ecuador upon her.

After this, Molly was given a new T-shirt with a smiling
skull on the front, and Gerry a yellow leather jacket that

Toka had recently grown out of. The mice were put away and then, ready for their supper with Mr Proila, the brothers and Molly, Gerry and Petula left the apartment.

As the glass lift descended, they saw Mr Proila and Miss Sny below. He had donned a white silk suit and was pacing up and down the lobby area, gesticulating madly.

When they drew level with him, they saw that he was talking on the phone and that his face was twisted with fury. The lift doors opened and they heard his gravelly voice shouting in a language Molly didn't recognize. Miss Sny was listening in on an extra handset so that she could tell Mr Proila in sign language what the person on the other end of the line was saying.

Mr Proila raised his eyes and, without pausing, looked away from Gerry, Molly and Petula, giving them as much attention as he might a stack of chairs.

Molly noticed that the top of the little finger on his right hand was missing. All that was left was a stump that twitched as he talked. And when he pulled his jacket sleeve back in exasperation at his stormy conversation, Molly saw that his arm was black as ink. In the next second she realized that this blackness was a tattoo. She wondered how far up his body it went. She saw a flash of tattoo on the skin under the collar of his shirt as well. He was obviously covered in them.

Beyond the door of the building a large chauffeur-driven limousine stood waiting. The usual crowds filled the pavement, and six bodyguards stood there like pillars.

When Mr Proila's phone call was over, he swaggered over to the children.

'So,' he began, addressing Hiroyuki disdainfully in his thick Russian accent. His voice was slightly loud even when he wasn't shouting; presumably his deafness meant he couldn't hear himself. 'These are your *little* friends –' an odd thing to say as he was so short himself. He pointed at Gerry – 'a hobo, a scruffball, a stinkball. Your old jacket, Toka, doesn't disguise that.' Turning to Molly he commented, 'This one can have her nose operated on as soon as she's fully grown. The surgeons can work wonders. But the eyes, too closely set. Nothing to be done about them, I'm afraid.'

Molly was momentarily stunned. No one had insulted her like this in a very long time. What with the mean grandmother and now with this rude man, Tokyo was beginning to feel hostile. But before she had time to think to turn her green eyes upon Mr Proila and let them ensnare him with hypnotism, he had put on his dark sunglasses and turned away.

'Sorry about his manners,' Chokichi said. 'He is perhaps the rudest person you will ever meet. Don't take it to heart. He is sick.'

'The good thing,' said Toka, 'is that you can talk behind his back and he can't hear what you say. Look!' Toka stepped up towards Mr Proila and said loudly, 'You are an ugly, stupid, rude toad, Proila . . . See?' He turned back to Molly.

But in the same instant Mr Proila's hand came

slamming down on Toka's shoulder. 'Not insulting me, I hope, Toka. I felt your step. Felt your breath, boy. Watch it!'

Toka shrank back towards his brothers.

Mr Proila and Miss Sny sat in the middle section of the limousine, partitioned from both the driver in the front and the children in the back as they drove to the restaurant, followed by two of the bodyguards in a car behind them.

'You're going to love this,' Chokichi said to Molly as they stopped.

Inside the triangular front door of the restaurant, three kimono-wearing hostesses greeted them, bowing low. Their lips were red, their cheeks were pink and each of them had their dark hair gathered in a bun decorated with sticks. Behind them was a giant fish tank. It covered the whole back wall, as high as the upper floor, where the restaurant's clients sat. Inside the tank was a rock garden with bright weed and colourful water flowers. Freshwater fish of all sorts – salmon, trout, carp and ayu – swam about in there, glooping and gliding. The hostesses presented them all with slippers.

All the children changed their shoes, as did Miss Sny. But Mr Proila ignored the slippers that were offered to him.

'Pah!' he spat, and, straightening his white jacket, he marched up the stairs.

The upstairs room was unbelievable. Most of the floor consisted of the surface of the fish tank Molly had seen downstairs, so it was like a large pond. It had five big wooden boats in it. The boats were fixed so that they were completely stable. Inside each was a long table, with enough space around it to seat twelve.

Chattering people sat at these, enjoying fish suppers – cooked or as sashimi (raw slices of fish, beautifully presented). Little flasks of Japanese sake wine and spouted bottles of soy sauce stood on the tables, and the people ate with wooden chopsticks. Everyone was relishing the novelty of the restaurant and this is why:

Fish swam in the water around the boats, and customers fished for their own supper. Once a fish had been caught, waiters took it to the chef, who killed, gutted and prepared it for eating.

On the furthest table, a young boy had just caught one. He was shielding his face as it struggled and flipped on the end of his line, splashing him. His family laughed as he grappled with the net.

'Horrid!' said Gerry disgustedly. 'Molly, you know I'm a vegetarian, don't you? I . . . I don't like killin' things and I 'specially don't like eating them.'

Molly put her hand to her mouth. 'Oh dear. Sorry, Gerry. Can you handle it? Maybe they have a vegetar—' But before she could ask for a vegetarian menu Mr Proila distracted her. He had started to shout at the restaurant's maître d'.

'NO! NO! I BOOKED TWO WHOLE TABLES! Who are these peasants on my table? Get them off it. If you don't get rid of them now, I will close this place down.

64

And, what's more, you will find yourself swimming around in that tank and being eaten for supper.'

The maître d' looked terrified. Cowering and obedient, he followed Mr Proila's orders.

'Mr Proila –' Hiroyuki stepped in front of his manager so that he could read his lips – 'we don't need two tables. Come on . . .' But Mr Proila flapped his hand irritatedly at Hiroyuki to shoo him away.

Once the table had been cleared, Mr Proila, like a horrid schoolboy who had just bullied a form full of kindergarten children, pushed his way to the best seat in the restaurant, at the end of one boat. Another big boat now sat empty beside it.

Rifling through the fishing rods there, Mr Proila chose what he obviously thought was the nicest for himself, dropping the others on the floor. Laughing in a showing-off way, as though everyone must surely be wanting to watch him have fun, he began casting his line.

'Come on!' he shouted to the band boys. 'COME ON, ZAGGER!'

The rest of the people in the restaurant now realized who the boys were. Silly fans that they were, they thought it quite appropriate that they should all clear the way for Hiroyuki, Chokichi and Toka and their party.

Embarrassed to have caused such a commotion, the boys found places to sit on the boats. Molly and Gerry and Petula sat down too. And everyone (except Gerry) found themselves a rod to use.

'COME ON, YOU SLIMY HORRORS!' Mr Proila

roared. 'LET'S SEE YOU!' He stood up and peered frustratedly into the pond. 'Where the hell are they? YOU HAVEN'T STOCKED YOUR POOL!' he yelled to the maître d'.

'Sir, we have,' the man replied, making sure Mr Proila could read his lips. 'You must be more quiet, then they will come.'

'*Quiet?!* What are you talking about? If this was my restaurant, I'd keep the fish so hungry that they'd be eating each other! I'd keep them so hungry that they'd come up and take the bait even if a rock concert was going on in here.'

'If we kept them that hungry,' the maître d' explained gently, 'there wouldn't be much flesh on them for you to eat when you caught them.'

Hiroyuki, Chokichi and Toka quietly got on with their fishing, ashamed of Mr Proila and the fuss he was making.

'Ridiculous!' Mr Proila spat. Then his phone, vibrating in his pocket, distracted him. He passed it to Miss Sny to take the call, then, turning to one of his bodyguards, said, 'Go to Fongi's. Get me some bluefin tuna. Don't want any of this boggy pond fish anyway.'

The bodyguard nodded and left at once. Mr Proila then got off the boat to march up and down the platform part of the restaurant, speaking with fierce intensity to Miss Sny who translated what he was saying to the person on the other end of the telephone line.

Molly, Hiroyuki, Chokichi and Toka each caught themselves a silvery fish and gave it to the waiter to prepare. Gerry looked very uncomfortable.

'Have you got any vegetarian food?' he asked a waiter.

'Certainly,' the man said. 'Sushi rolls with cucumber, and vegetable tempura – that's vegetables fried in batter.'

'That sounds nice.' Gerry was relieved.

'Do you always eat out?' Molly asked Chokichi as they waited for their food.

'It depends on Mr Proila,' Chokichi replied. 'Sometimes he goes out on his own, but if he wants us about we have to jump to it.'

'Like a controlling parent,' said Molly, thinking of Lucy and Primo.

'No, he's not like a parent at all,' Chokichi replied. 'He doesn't love us. He just loves the money we make for him.'

Molly nodded. For some reason, the way she felt at the moment, this didn't seem a bad arrangement at all. Then she asked curiously, 'How did he get to the top? I mean, everyone seems scared stiff of him. Even though he's so small, and deaf. People could just pick him up and throw him over their shoulder, or his enemies could say things behind his back. It's amazing he's as powerful as he is.'

Chokichi nodded. 'Being small doesn't matter. He's got four very loyal and very big bodyguards. He pays them lot of money. And with deafness – Mr Proila was not always deaf. He was in a shootout.'

'A shootout? Really?'

'Yes. To save Mr Proila's life his bodyguard fired some gunshots, but guard's gun was very close to Mr Proila's ears. Burst his eardrums. Three years ago.'

'What happened to that bodyguard?' Molly asked.

Chokichi checked to see that Mr Proila wasn't lip-reading him. 'Nobody know,' he said. 'He disappear. Mr Proila say he move away, but nobody know for sure.'

Molly nodded, her hand on her coin. Strangely, she was beginning to admire Mr Proila.

Petula watched her mistress. Again that acrid, bitter-lemon smell was coming from Molly. It was a smell that made Petula feel queasy and very uneasy. Petula sidled closer to Gerry. She was scared by whatever was happening to Molly, but most of all she was saddened. Saddened because her instinct was to keep away from Molly, and this felt unnatural, for Petula still loved her mistress. She didn't know what to do.

The waiter brought miso soup for everyone. Mr Proila returned to the table, grunted, sat down heavily on the end of the bench and started slurping his soup.

When his bodyguard returned, he was carrying a very smart red paper bag with gold lines around its edges. Without thanking him, Mr Proila took the bag and peered inside. He pulled out a red box and flipped its lid open. Snapping apart the chopsticks that had come in the bag too, he began pincering out pieces of pale pink marbled flesh from the red box and eating them.

'*Otoro!* My favourite!' he said with a full mouth. 'Best, most delicious fish in the world!' he said, gobbling up his supper. Then he saw that Gerry was glaring at him. 'What ya staring at, boy?'

Gerry looked furious. Molly wondered what could have caused his anger.

Gerry stood up and pointed at Mr Proila's meal box. 'How can you eat that?' he said coldly.

Mr Proila squinted as he read Gerry's lips. 'With great pleasure, that's how!' he laughed, showing a mouthful of half-chewed fish.

'But that fish . . . bluefin tuna – is rare. It is endangered. Eating bluefin tuna is like eating tiger meat or rhino!'

'Wouldn't mind a tiger steak!' came Mr Proila's amused reply.

He scrutinized Gerry, so small and opinionated and cross at the end of the table, and he guffawed and then bellowed with laughter. But as his mouth was still full of chewed fish, a bit down went down his windpipe. This sent him into spasms of coughing. For a moment the coughing was still accompanied by laughter, then, as he grew puce in the face and his bodyguard patted him on the back, he grew more serious. When he had finally rid himself of the cough and his breathing had levelled out, his sense of humour had vanished. As though the coughing fit had been all Gerry's doing, he gave him a nasty look and pointed his chopsticks at him.

'Listen, tadpole,' he said, 'and listen good. First of all, what I do is no business of anyone's except mine. If you ever talk to me like that again, I'll sushi you. And, as for the tuna, I don't care if it's the absolute last bluefin in the sea. I get what I want, and if I want bluefin tuna, I'll eat it.'

Gerry looked stunned. He sat down, shaken. Petula jumped up on his knee to comfort him. Hiroyuki, Chokichi and Toka patted his back reassuringly. Molly went to sit beside him. She put a hand on his shoulder. Half of her knew she ought to stick up for Gerry, but the other half didn't care enough to.

'Don't worry about it, Gerry,' she said under her breath. 'But you shouldn't have wound him up.'

Gerry stood up. 'I'm going to the toilet,' he announced. 'To be sick!' he added.

'I come with you,' Toka said.

Chapter Eleven

Molly watched Gerry and Toka go, then turned her attention back to Mr Proila. Her hand strayed into her pocket. She touched her gold coin and, as she did, a curious impulse overwhelmed her – to take her harmonica from her other pocket and play it. Molly pressed the instrument to her lips and with a deep breath began to play. Only a small part of her wondered why she was doing this.

Hiroyuki and Chokichi looked up. The notes from Molly's mouth organ danced through the air. Molly could certainly play the small instrument. As its metallic melody filled the restaurant, Hiroyuki and Chokichi became immersed in the sound. Miss Sny tipped her head to listen too. People at other tables looked up. The waiters halted what they were doing. Even the bodyguards gazed at Molly as the marvellous sound rippled into the air.

The music she was making was fantastic, like something heaven-sent. And, Molly noticed, the more she played, the more in awe her audience was.

Petula sat on the second table boat, away from Molly. Molly was smelling ever stronger – now of sharp thorns and poisonous flowers. Petula knew that normally Molly had no musical skills. Yet here she was, as though she had been born playing a harmonica – as though she had been taught to play it by the angels.

As Petula looked about, she saw the effect the music was having on the humans in the restaurant. They seemed mesmerized by the sound. Petula squeezed her eyes and checked herself. No, she was definitely not hypnotized. But it was clear to her that everyone in the restaurant, except for Mr Proila, who was eating a chocolate dessert, was. This music Molly was making was hypnotic in a way more powerful than Molly's hypnotic eyes could ever be. For this hypnotism was effective en masse. If there had been a thousand people in the room, Petula knew that they all would have been affected by this music.

Petula knew that this sudden musical ability, and Molly's new meanness, were both connected to the coin; the foul-smelling, evil-feeling coin that Petula could sense right now in Molly's pocket.

When Molly finished her piece the customers and the waiters let out cheers of appreciation. Everyone was smitten. Everyone that is, bar Mr Proila, who was wiping his mouth with a napkin.

Chokichi shook Mr Proila's arm.

'Mr Proila,' he said, making sure his manager could read his lips, 'Molly's an amazing musician!'

Mr Proila looked up from his dessert and saw the enthused faces about him. He studied the waiters' gleeful expressions and he saw that the object of everyone's enthusiasm was the plain-looking girl with the scruffy hair who held a mouth organ in her hand. Mr Proila had never cared for music, even when he had been able to hear, but he was very interested in the money he could make from it.

'I've an idea, Mr Proila,' Chokichi said. 'Why doesn't she play with us at the concert tomorrow night? She's great. The audience will love her.'

Mr Proila had been in the music business long enough to know a hot thing when it sizzled in front of him. Regardless of what the potato-nosed girl looked like, it was quite obvious from the faces of the people in the restaurant that whatever she did on her harmonica was hot. He shrugged his shoulders and nodded.

'Of course,' he said nonchalantly. 'Good idea.'

Then, deciding that one pudding hadn't been enough, he waved at the waiter to bring him the dessert menu.

When Gerry and Toka returned to the table, Petula could tell they hadn't heard any of Molly's music – and they hadn't been hypnotized. Did Molly know what she had done to the others? She must do, Petula thought, for Molly was experienced enough to know what hypnotized people looked like. Then Petula wondered whether Molly had even registered that Gerry and Toka had been absent.

Petula began to shiver with worry. Somehow she must protect Gerry and Toka from this new Molly and her dangerous music.

She thought of the coin that sat like an evil imp in Molly's pocket. Petula knew what she must do. She must get the coin.

The rest of the evening passed quickly. They piled into the limousine once more and were soon back at the apartment.

Gerry was exhausted, and he and Toka went upstairs to bed. Petula hid under a chair and watched Molly pacing the lounge with the coin in her hand. Petula was sure she overheard her whispering to it.

More frightened than sad now, Petula crept up the stairs to Toka's room. She hopped on to Gerry's bed and curled up there.

Molly sat on a stool beside the window. She stroked her coin. 'To think I've been carrying you about without realizing until this evening what you can do,' she whispered to it. 'All that power sitting in my pocket! You are amazing. You make me amazing.'

All of a sudden a flickering to her right caught her attention. She glanced up quickly, at the same time automatically closing her hand over her coin.

Someone had just jumped over the edge of the balcony outside. Molly put the coin on the table and went to check that the balcony door was locked.

She pressed her nose to the glass and tried to see into the darkness.

'Pick me up,' a voice whispered behind her.

Molly's eyes shot to the grandmother's hiding place. So the old lady spoke English! Molly tentatively approached the space under the stairs, but when she got there she found it was empty.

'Pick me up, Molly!'

Molly swung round. Her eyes fell on the coin. This was the first time she'd put the coin down in the open. It was obviously not happy.

It was not happy . . . ? *It?* Molly must be going mad. For it was a coin, that was all. She must have imagined it talking to her. Yet she knew she hadn't.

For the first time since the coin had been in her possession, Molly was startled and shocked by it. Suddenly she became acutely aware that it was somehow like a person – a very powerful, controlling person – a person that was trying to change her.

A film started running in her mind, one about all the bad things she had done over the last few days. Molly observed her behaviour. She'd been horrible to Micky. She'd even hypnotized him. She'd hurt her parents' feelings and she'd not helped Gerry in the restaurant when Mr Proila had been mean to him. She'd ignored Petula. In fact, she'd been spiteful to her and scared her. All because of this thing on the table, because of this coin.

Trembling, Molly reached for the phone and dialled the number for Briersville.

'Hello?' came Rocky's comforting, warm voice.

'Rocky, it's me.'

'Molly! Where are you? Are you OK? Primo and Lucy are tearing their hair out. They've gone to Ecuador to find you. They're on the plane right now. Are you all right?'

Molly could feel the coin tugging at her. Now it was calling her in a different way, with thin, harp-like music that she couldn't ignore. A music that seemed to tear at her will and prevent her saying what she meant to.

'Come to Tokyo now,' she managed to say. 'Please. Next plane.'

'Molly, what's wrong? Has something happened? Where are you?'

'Pea-pod Building. There's a band called Zagger. I'm with them.' As Molly spoke, tears welled up in her eyes. The coin on the table was beginning to send more than messages and music to Molly. It now seemed to have looped her with an invisible lasso. 'Rocky, I don't know what I'll be like when you come. There's a c-c . . .'

'NOOOOO!' the coin whispered fiercely. 'Don't give me away. You need me, Molly.'

'A what?' Rocky asked frantically.

'Come!' Molly begged, starting to pant from the effort of resisting the coin. 'Hurry, Rocky. Before it's too late!'

As though a spirit had hold of her, the coin swamped Molly's whole being. It took control of her hand. Without wanting to, Molly found her finger pressing the 'end call' button.

Molly was sweating. Her brow was damp and her lips were dry. The coin started to sing to her more loudly now, embracing her.

'Come on, Molly!' it sang. 'We could be marvellous together. The world will be ours!'

Molly found herself walking towards the table, overwhelmed. She picked it up.

At once she felt wonderful. It was a feeling of perfect joining, like when two pieces of puzzle slot beautifully together, but multiplied hundreds of times. All the guilt she had felt just moments before evaporated, as did her feeling of needing Rocky.

'I'm sorry,' she apologized to the coin. 'I was a fool. I won't leave you out in the open again. Please will you forgive me?'

Chapter Twelve

Petula woke early the next morning, and immediately switched to high alert. She stayed by Gerry's side at breakfast, determined to protect him from Molly. She sat sentry-like outside the bathroom while he was taking a shower. But it was soon obvious that Molly was far too distracted to think of playing her mouth organ.

Mr Proila had agreed that Molly could do a short slot as a guest performer at Zagger's concert that night at the Tokyo Dome. A costume had to be made for her. And so a team had arrived – a designer, and a seamstress – bearing bags filled with materials and accessories.

Molly was desperate for the evening to come. The fun of choosing her costume eased the waiting and she picked out some long leather boots to complete her look. The design team hurried off, promising to have Molly's outfit back by six.

'Oh, by the way,' Molly announced when they were all eating lunch, 'a boy called Rocky will be turning up later today. Not sure what time.' She didn't ask whether her hosts minded, as she knew they were already under her power. She must get Rocky under her influence at the first opportunity too. He would be trouble otherwise. She would leave hypnotizing Gerry until then, as otherwise Gerry's adoration of Molly might make Rocky suspicious.

'Rocky!' Gerry cried. 'Wow! Cool! Is it OK if he stays here, Toka? He's really nice.'

Petula, who was perched on a chair a little distance away, studied Molly's every move, checking that she didn't reach for her mouth organ again.

Petula knew for sure that, more than tarnishing Molly's manners, the coin was poisoning her spirit. Petula had seen the coin work its evil effect before – in the hands of the foul Miss Hunroe. Miss Hunroe's greed had showed no bounds. She had obliterated any obstacle that stood in her way. Her idea of a perfect world had been one where most people would be wiped out. Petula wondered whether Miss Hunroe had been good to start with, before she owned the coin? Until recently Molly had used her amazing powers in the right way. But might she now become a heartless monster? With all her basic talents corrupted by the gold coin, Molly could be really dangerous.

Molly took the coin from her pocket and flipped it through her fingers. It was then that Petula made a decision. She would steal the thing this afternoon. Molly slept with the coin under her pillow. The more attached to it she became, the less chance there was of her leaving it unattended. But she would, and when she did Petula would be ready. Until then she would do everything she could to stop Molly playing her mouth organ. In fact, if she possibly could, she would steal that from Molly too.

Petula's chance came when Molly's costume was brought back. The pug sat on the mezzanine balcony outside the boys' bedroom. Molly was so excited to see her outfit that she came rushing out of the spare room below. As soon as Molly appeared, the old grandmother wheeled herself backwards into her dark, shadowy corner. Petula looked down and noticed that Molly wasn't wearing her black jacket, which probably meant that the coin and the mouth organ were in the bedroom still, in the jacket's pockets.

Petula quietly picked her way down the stairs. As Molly was removing her shoes and whooping with delight as she pulled on the glossy new boots, Petula slipped into her room.

The room was dark. The curtains were shut. It took a few moments for Petula's eyes to adjust. A glow emanated from the TV screen. Molly had been watching a movie and had paused it. A picture of a vampire sucking blood from a young boy's neck was frozen there. It reminded Petula how much Molly had changed – the old Molly hadn't liked scary films at all. The picture on the screen accompanied by the bitter smell of the coin gave Petula the creeps.

She trotted over to the curtains. Using her forehead and shoulders she parted them a bit to let some light in. The jacket lay across the unmade bed. Petula could smell the coin inside it. Better still, the mouth organ was on the bedside table. Petula put her mouth up to the table, took the instrument and posted it under the bed. She jumped up on to the duvet and with her paw swiped at the jacket to expose the lining. The coin was in an inner pocket. It was practically breathing. Live as a demon or an evil scorpion, it sat smug and malevolent. What really scared Petula was that she felt sure that it, this horrid entity residing in gold, was aware of her. Her skin prickled and the hair on her neck bristled. Petula shook her ears and head.

Now, as she looked, darkness seemed to swirl about the pocket where the coin was. Was she imagining it? Steeling her nerves, Petula slid her paw into the pocket.

And then a really weird thing happened. She could not touch the coin. She knew it was there, but her paw could not make contact with it. It was as if the coin had a shield that kept it safe from thieves, or certainly from her. No matter how hard she tried, Petula simply could not touch it. She withdrew her paw. She would have to drag the jacket somewhere and hide it. Then Molly wouldn't be able to find it, and perhaps the coin's evil influence would wane. Gripping the jacket's collar with her teeth, Petula began to tug, but found the jacket was stuck. It was as if it was staked to the bed.

Petula was tugging so hard that she didn't notice a creaking, squeaking noise behind her. When she looked up, she nearly yelped in fright. The grandmother in her wheelchair was staring at her. Half certain that she was something to do with the evil coin too, Petula backed off.

However, the old lady nodded at Petula encouragingly. Leaning forward in her wheelchair, she dipped her gnarled hand into Molly's jacket pocket. Her arm began to shake, then her face to twist as she attempted to close her fingers around the coin. The veins in her scrawny neck stood out as she concentrated on trying to force her hand to close. And then, as though she had received a massive electric shock, she cried out in pain. Her hand shot back towards herself and she bent over to nurse it. The coin was still in the pocket.

At the same moment, they both noticed that Molly stood in the doorway. She was wearing shiny black leather boots, a black velvet miniskirt and a silver jacket. Her black T-shirt had a skull on it – but not the smiley skull of before. She marched up to the bed and picked up the jacket easily. Putting her hand into the pocket, she retrieved her coin. Petula could practically hear the golden object purr. Molly leaned forward and poked Petula hard. Then, roughly, she brushed her off the bed. Next she grabbed the wheelchair. Smiling with saccharin sweetness, she turned the grandmother to the door and shoved her out of the room.

Petula sat dazed and confused on the floor. Everything was out of control. She must save the real Molly, but she didn't know how.

Suddenly she was afraid of what Molly might do if she

discovered her mouth organ missing. If she guessed Petula had hidden it, she might be so livid that she would call the dog pound. Petula couldn't let this happen. In the pound she'd be no use to anyone. With a swipe of her paw she reluctantly retrieved the harmonica from under the bed and left it visible on the floor.

Molly came back through the door, putting the coin in the pocket of her silver jacket. She studied Petula and picked up her harmonica. Then, as disgusted as she might be by a rat that had fleas all over it, she whispered viciously, 'GET OUT!'

Petula's ears flattened and, scared to the core, she bolted for the door.

It was odd, Molly thought as she watched her go. Once she had had warm feelings for Petula, but now she couldn't care less about her. She had grown up, she supposed – her affection for Petula had been a childish thing. The pug was just a dog. The feelings she'd had for Petula now seemed insipid and sickly, sugary and fake. She shivered with revulsion as she thought of them. And now Molly thought about the amount of time she had spent over the last few years caring about other people. Again, it made her squirm with sickness.

Molly saw now that somehow she had got things completely wrong. She was a fabulous hypnotist and, provided she had her special crystals, a time stopper and time traveller. She was amazing! She was even a morpher. She could change into any creature she chose and, to cap it all, she could read minds. But until now, like a fool, she'd used her gifts to help other people.

Curiously though, she didn't feel inclined to use her old talents. The coin could help her mesmerize crowds of people. It gave her something far superior to her other powers. People weren't hypnotized one by one in the way that they were when she used her eyes. They weren't in a trance where they would instantly obey her every command. But they were mesmerized into being totally besotted by Molly. Perhaps with more intense music people would be more deeply hypnotized. Molly was looking forward to trying that. Regular hypnotism might come in useful for certain situations, she thought, but this mesmerizing harmonica music was potentially much more useful to her. She'd be able to make a fortune.

Molly sat on the edge of the bed and took the coin from her pocket. She marvelled at how musical skill had come to her so easily. It was miraculous and brilliant. But there was another thing this music had done too. By being perfect when she played the mouth organ, Molly had become hyper-aware of the imperfections about her. Anything ugly or wrong got on her nerves, and that included people. In one fell swoop she had become a connoisseur of perfection. So, for instance, her new boots were perfect and made her feel good. But her suitcase, sitting there in the corner of the room, was worn out and old. She wanted a sophisticated Italian suitcase, of crocodile skin.

She ought to have the best of everything. The best clothes, the best electrical equipment, the best art should surround her. The furniture she sat on, the cars she was driven in, the food she ate should be nothing but the best. She deserved it. And the people around her had a duty to make her life better too. Anyone who disapproved of her or disappointed her shouldn't be there. Petula, for instance, and Gerry. Irritating Gerry, with his self-righteous ideals and his stupid 'Save the Whales or Else' T-shirt and his dirty mouse.

The old grandmother? Well, Molly hoped she would have a heart attack. As for Mr Proila, he was the most worthwhile person about. He would make sure Molly succeeded. And how she wanted to succeed! The boy band she would tolerate. She needed them, for now.

Molly smiled happily. Tonight was going to be bliss. Thousands of people would hear her play. They would all love her. Worship her! This thought calmed her. She put the harmonica to her mouth and blew. The flawless music she made gave her complete satisfaction. It was the best feeling ever.

She lay back on her bed and fell asleep.

Molly dreamed. She dreamed of a girl that looked like her but whose face was worried and whose voice was irritating. The girl was on a beach, standing at the bottom of a deep pit. Molly, at the top of the pit, played a guitar. People walked past and smiled and clapped adoringly. Each time they burst into applause the pit with the other girl in it got deeper. As she descended, the girl's bleatings grew more and more distant. 'I'm the real Molly!' the girl cried out.

Molly woke with a start and immediately felt for her coin. Reassured by its comforting presence, she rolled over and went back to sleep.

The girl was, of course, herself.

Chapter Thirteen

There was frenetic excitement in the apartment. Everyone was preparing to leave for the concert.

The grandmother and Miss Shonyo came to the door to see the children off. Sobo kissed her grandsons and gave each of them and Gerry and Molly a rectangular silk bag.

'It's an *omamori*,' Chokichi explained. 'It has a prayer written on wood or paper tucked inside it. The prayer is to bring good luck, or ward off bad luck. The string at the top is so you can tie it to you.'

Molly looked at her *omamori* as though it was a dried frog.

Passing the screaming crowds outside the Pea-pod Building, Hiroyuki, Chokichi and Molly got into the first limo. Petula hung back with Gerry and Toka. They climbed into the second car.

'Are you excited?' Gerry asked Toka. 'You don't look like you're feelin' well.'

'I hate going onstage. I feel sick to my stomach every time. My legs go weak. I *hate* it.'

Gerry patted Toka on the arm. 'That's bad,' he said. 'You should try an' sort that out. Remember, they all love you. And you're a really good drummer.'

'Thanks, Gerry. But I can't change my nerves. In sumo match it would be different. One day I'll be sumo wrestler. Then no nerves.'

Gerry looked surprised. 'Is that your dream, to be a sumo wrestler?'

'As soon as Proila let me, I will do it.'

The stadium was a vast place: silvery, with metal struts and flying buttresses up its sides. Gerry thrust his nose against the window. 'Wow! Look at the size of this place!'

'It takes about forty thousand people. We usually pack it out.'

'Wow!' Gerry gasped again. 'To have to entertain so many people!'

Toka nodded grimly.

Ten minutes later the children sat in a luxurious dressing room. Vertical rows of light bulbs shone out from the mirrors behind a row of dressing tables laden with make-up. Spectacular costumes hung on a rail.

'How do you decide what to wear?' Molly asked.

'It depends on the show we're doing,' said Chokichi. 'We have a list of different acts with different songs

88

and different routines. What set are we doing tonight, Hiroyuki?'

Hiroyuki consulted a piece of paper on the dressing table.

'He wants us to do number four, with three of the new songs too.'

'And when do I come on?' Molly asked.

Hiroyuki looked at the paper again. 'At end.'

'Wow, Molly!' Gerry said enthusiastically. 'I can't believe you're actually going onstage to play that harmonica I got you!'

Molly shrugged. 'And where is Mr Proila? Is he going to be watching?' Molly had her hands in both of her pockets. Her fingers turned her coin and her mouth organ over and over.

'Yes.' Chokichi cracked open a bottle of water. 'From a special glass box on the side of stadium. He like to watch the crowd's reaction. He hates music, but like we told you, he likes the money music make him.'

Gerry, with Petula curled up on his knees, sat in a big swivel chair. Petula stared at Molly's pocket. She wished with all her heart that Molly would leave her mouth organ there. If she brought it out to play, Petula wasn't sure she'd be able to stop herself from running at Molly and biting her hand.

'You know what?' Gerry said. 'Petula feels a bit nervous to me. I don't want to leave her all alone.'

'You could take her with you and sit on the edge of the stage with Molly,' Chokichi said. 'Perfect view.'

Gerry tilted his head. 'Maybe. OK then.'

Toka slumped down on a chair next to him. He turned his sequinned costume over in his hands. 'Look at this stupid outfit. I hate being pop star. I would prefer eat rotten eggs. An' I feel so sick, Gerry – like I have eaten rotten eggs.' Suddenly he got up. 'Excuse me.' He disappeared through a door into the adjoining room.

'That's the bathroom,' explained Chokichi. 'He's throwing up. By the time he gets onstage he'll be so wiped out from being ill that he won't be nervous.'

Molly went to the fridge and pulled out a fizzy drink. She cared as much about Toka's problems as a hyena might about a zebra's.

The time for the show drew closer. The brothers put on their first costumes: red winged outfits. Make-up and hair technicians came in. Molly was made up too.

The dressing room's soundproof door was opened. Immediately a swell of noise – the frenzied clapping and cheering of an expectant crowd filled the air.

Molly walked behind all the boys, cool as a cool breeze.

'Good luck!' Gerry called after them.

The curtain of the Tokyo Dome stage opened and the boy band were on. Holding his sticks in the air, Toka knocked themtogether. *TAP, TAP, TAP*. The microphone picked up the sound.

'*KONICHIWA*, TOKYO! And hello to everybody who isn't Japanese too!' Hiroyuki nodded particularly to Molly, who was sitting a little distance from Gerry and Petula on the edge of the stage. 'Hope you enjoy show!'

The show was even more spectacular than the one in Ecuador. The boys sang and danced, electrifying the packed, adoring crowd. One unforeseen happening was Toka excusing himself from the stage because he felt so ill – but the audience was sympathetic and Chokichi took over some of the drumming. As they finished their last song, Hiroyuki took the microphone.

Hiroyuki thrust his arm out at Gerry, who was sitting on a seat with Petula on his lap, and beamed at them. 'Meet Gerry, and Petula,' he said in English.

Gerry looked appalled to have so much attention focused on him. Uncertainly he picked up Petula's paw and made her wave to the crowd. This caused a massive response.

'OOOOH!'

'AAAAHHH!'

Gerry blushed and shook as the audience clapped. He got up. Awkwardly he bowed, then he waved. But his wave wasn't one of greeting – it was a goodbye. Walking as fast as he could without appearing to be rude, Gerry left the stage.

Hiroyuki explained to the crowd that Gerry was shy and that he'd probably gone off to see Toka. The audience clapped some more.

'And now we have surprise for you, ' he said. 'Our guest today! Meet Molly Moon!'

Molly stood up. She strode over to join the boys and smiled at the crowd. She dipped her hand into her pocket.

'Molly,' Chokichi explained, 'is AMAZING on the mouth organ. Aren't you, Molly?'

Molly could have shrugged and said something modest, but instead she replied conceitedly, 'You bet. I'm the best!'

The audience laughed, thinking she was joking, and then she began.

She started with a huge blow, making her harmonica sound like some sort of groovy locomotive whistle. Then she stopped and leaned towards the microphone. 'The music train is coming,' she said coldly.

Again the audience read her wrongly, thinking her iciness was an act. Molly started again. The audience began to clap and sway. Each person, without knowing it, was becoming a passenger on Molly's hypnotic train.

As soon as Molly finished, a tsunami of awe-inspired applause crashed over her.

Hiroyuki and Chokichi beamed at Molly. She smiled back. She stepped towards Chokichi's silver guitar and picked it off its rack.

'May I?' she asked.

With an amazed look on his face, Chokichi nodded. Molly hitched the guitar's strap over her head and made herself comfortable with the instrument. The audience hushed in anticipation.

Molly couldn't play the guitar, but she remembered that the Molly on the beach in her dream had been able to play the guitar perfectly. She had no idea how the frets worked, how to get a good sound from it – and yet she felt an urge to play it. The electric guitar was such a gorgeously cool instrument that it would be a pity if she could not get a good sound from it.

If her new-found musical ability didn't stretch to mastering the guitar, that was fine, she thought. She would simply pretend that she was fooling around and then she'd go back to the harmonica. Yet she had a feeling it would work.

Molly let her finger pluck out three notes. It felt good. Her fingers seemed to know what they were doing. She plucked six more notes and then, without her thinking about it, the fingers on her left hand changed position, pressing down on the guitar's fretboard as though they had a mind of their own. Molly's right hand strummed. The left hand moved again, and Molly's right hand strummed faster. And then the music took off. Molly was phenomenal. It was the best guitar music that anyone in the Tokyo Dome had ever heard. Molly made the guitar talk. She made it sing. She was astounding. The audience was spellbound.

She knew the end of her piece was coming. She stared out into the crowd and smiled with satisfaction, getting ready for the glory that she knew awaited her. She let her fingers fly and a crescendo of notes filled the air. Then she flung her hand away from the guitar in a gesture of finality – Molly was finished.

At first the audience was so enamoured by Molly that it was stunned. Then it blew its top. The applause was so full of screams that it sounded like a flock of alien birds had possessed the stadium.

If the audience had known what had really just happened to them, their cries might well have been screams of fear, but they had no idea that Molly's music had hypnotized them.

Molly was fast becoming a monster. She had no feelings for the thousands of people before her. She simply wanted their adoration and their money. She bowed. Then she raised her eyes to the glass box that hung at the edge of one of the stands. She could see Mr Proila there. He was standing up, observing the crowd and puffing on a fat cigar. He looked at Molly. Molly nodded slowly at him. She gestured towards the audience as if to say, 'Now do you see what I can do?' But she didn't need to point anything out. Mr Proila had already seen the effect she had had. Although he'd not heard a note from Molly of course, he could see the crowd's reaction.

'She's genius!' Miss Sny insisted, making sure Mr Proila could read her mouth.

Back in the dressing room, Gerry and Toka were watching a martial-arts film with Petula beside them. They had missed the performance. When Molly came back, she hardly noticed them. Adrenalin pumped through her as she reeled from her new thrilling power.

'You were great! I mean, truly great,' Hiroyuki declared. 'They loved you. They definitely want to see you more, Molly. You could be really big.'

'I should be,' Molly declared.

'Definitely,' agreed Chokichi.

'You could take my place in the band,' suggested Toka. 'I'd love it if you did that.'

Molly smiled. Things were moving in the right direction, she thought. But she didn't want Toka's place. She wanted more than that.

'Did you all play together?' Gerry asked.

Molly noticed Gerry now, rather like a cat might notice a flea on its fur.

'No,' she said coldly. 'I played the harmonica and then I played the guitar. Both times on my own.'

'Can you play the guitar too, now?' Gerry asked incredulously. 'That's amazin'. When I last saw you, you couldn't play nothin'.'

'Well, you wondered what I'd been doing,' Molly quipped. 'I've picked up quite a few instruments,' she lied. It struck her that other instruments would definitely work for her too. 'You'll see.'

Gerry looked impressed. Then he sighed. 'You know what, Petula's tired. So am I. Can we go back to the hotel soon?'

Molly shrugged. The truth was, she didn't care what Gerry or Petula got up to now.

'Sure.'

Just then the door burst open.

Mr Proila, white-suited and smoking a cigar, stood in the doorway, his hands on his hips. He blew smoke into the room. Then he stepped in. Miss Sny trotted behind him, her eyes glowing with admiration for Molly.

'Not bad,' Mr Proila said casually to the boys. Then, careful not to look too enthusiastic, he added glibly, 'And, Miss Moon – they seemed to like you a bit too.'

'A bit?' Hiroyuki blurted out. He stepped in front of Mr Proila so that he could read his lips. 'They loved her, Mr Proila.'

Mr Proila sucked at his cigar. He carelessly puffed the grey nicotine cloud of burnt tobacco into Hiroyuki's face. 'They'll forget her soon enough if she isn't marketed properly,' he replied scathingly. 'I've seen kids like her – acts that thought the world was their oyster, until the oyster clamped shut, leaving 'em nothing but barnacles and mud. It's one thing hitting the top, it's quite another staying there. If Molly wants the big time, she needs me.'

Molly smiled knowingly.

''Scuse,' Gerry interrupted, tapping Mr Proila's arm, 'but would it be all right for us to have a car now to go home?'

Mr Proila sneered at him. 'You again? The defender of the fish.' He grimaced and screwed up his eyes as he read Gerry's T-shirt. '"Save the Whales or Else"? Else what, shrimp?' He began to laugh, then to wind Gerry up he added, 'By the way, somebody informed me that the evil bluefin-tuna dealer will be at the Tsukiji Fish Market tomorrow. You want to stop him dealing it? You need to catch him!'

Gerry frowned at Mr Proila. 'What do you mean?'

But Mr Proila had turned away. 'So, boys,' he was saying, 'I feel like going out tonight.'

'But we're tired,' said Hiroyuki. 'It's been a big night, Mr Proila.'

'No,' their manager insisted. 'You need to hang out with me.'

Hanging out sounded scary when Mr Proila said it. For a moment there was quiet as the boys hesitated. Mr Proila was a bad-tempered man. None of them dared refuse him. Then Molly spoke up. 'I'll hang out with you,' she said.

Mr Proila eyed Molly. 'Well, if these killjoys can't take it, it's you and me. Come on then.'

He turned on his Cuban heels and pushed past the others. Miss Sny bobbed along behind him.

Molly shrugged. Without a word, she followed Mr Proila out.

Chapter Fourteen

Mr Proila's red sports car glided, a red pearl over velvet, through the streets of Tokyo. Molly leaned back into the passenger seat. Miss Sny was cramped into the small space behind.

Molly tapped her host on the shoulder and asked him where they were going, but he didn't bother answering her. Molly didn't mind. She quite enjoyed his rudeness, because, frankly, she felt rude herself. She didn't want to talk to him either. When they turned from skyscraper-lined streets to a scruffier, more characterful neon-lit neighbourhood and the streets got darker and dirtier, Molly wasn't scared. Her hypnotism was so good that she knew she would easily be able to get out of any trouble. She'd heard of girls her age being kidnapped and sold as slaves, but she knew Mr Proila wasn't about to do that. It was obvious he knew that he could make millions and millions from Molly. She could practically see the yen signs in his eyes when he looked at her. And the great thing was he was so corrupt that he had no worries about who Molly was or where she came from. He hadn't asked. She knew he'd go along with any lie she told him.

Mr Proila pulled up in front of a dingy warehouse with a stone facade. Two mean-looking, thick-set bouncers stood guarding a rusty double door.

'Now for some fun!' Mr Proila declared, rubbing his little hands together. He and Molly climbed out of the car, Miss Sny clambering after them. Mr Proila's bodyguards got out of the black Mercedes that had been following them. The bouncers opened the metal warehouse door and stood aside for Mr Proila as though he was some kind of king. Molly ignored them, as was her way now. She felt superior to everyone.

The noise inside was a surprise. A swell of voices and shouts peppered by, 'GO! GO! *Ikut!*' filled the air. Then there was a roaring cheer. Mr Proila led Molly and Miss Sny along a dark passage that smelt of sweat and sawdust.

Ahead were red curtains that concealed the source of the clamour. Mr Proila parted the drapes and went through, letting them swing back to block Molly's way. Miss Sny immediately leaped forward and opened them for her.

Beyond was a room about as wide and as long as three small trucks. In its centre was a sunken square floor with platforms round it. These wide platforms went up for three steps on each side. Each had a rail along the front of it so that the people standing there didn't fall forward into the arena, which was strewn with sawdust – sawdust that had soaked up some sort of dark liquid. The room had filthy walls and was lit by six bare bulbs hanging from the ceiling. There must have been about a hundred and fifty people in the room, ranging from businessmen in shirtsleeves and loosened ties to brawny dockers in stained string vests. There were a few women too, all hard-looking with mean eyes.

An elderly man in a black shirt and wearing grey braces to hold up his trousers, stood, feet apart, in the middle of the arena. He raised his voice to make an announcement to the crowd.

At the back of the room, along the walls, pairs of men in white shirts and blue trousers stood in front of boards with Japanese writing on them. One man in each of the pairs seemed to be in charge of changing the writing on the board, while the other wrote chits out for a queue of frantic customers who waved money as though they needed to buy something that would save their lives.

They were betting, Molly realized, though on what, she didn't know. The lowered area was surely too small for boxers.

Mr Proila led them to a high platform at the edge of the room.

'Up,' he said to Molly, and she climbed the narrow steps after him. Miss Sny, knowing her place, stayed obediently at the bottom beside one of the bodyguards. She looked apprehensive, flattening herself against the back wall of the room as if she'd like to disappear.

The bodyguard stood aside to let a man come up the steps, and after a brief chat with Mr Proila he wrote a chit for him. Mr Proila, in turn, passed him a thick wad of notes.

'What are you betting on?' Molly asked.

'Tell me first,' Mr Proila said, watching Molly's lips to read them, 'red or black?'

'Black,' Molly decided.

'OK.' Mr Proila spoke to the man again. Another chit was written and more money changed hands. Mr Proila passed Molly the piece of paper. 'For you. I put down sixty-six thousand yen for you. If black wins, you win two hundred thousand yen. Feeling lucky?'

Molly shrugged, and took the chit. She tried to calculate in her head. Sixty-six thousand yen was a lot of money. She was sure that two hundred thousand yen was more than a thousand pounds! Mr Proila was obviously a keen gambler.

In front of them, the audience was starting to get impatient. People waved their betting slips and were beginning to stamp the ground.

'*TATAKAU! TATAKAU! TATAKAU!*' they shouted.

'What are they shouting?' Molly asked Mr Proila.

'"*Tatakau*" means "fight",' Mr Proila replied.

Again the crowd clamoured: '*TATAKAU! TATAKAU!*'

In the next moment there was a cheer. Two men climbed down ladders and placed metal cages on the floor in the centre of the sawdust-strewn arena. Another man, a fierce-looking bearded brute in a white tunic, came on. He held an orange flag above his head. When he brought this down, the handlers opened the cages.

Two cockerels sprang out. One had a red ribbon around its neck, the other a black one.

'This is where the fun starts . . .' Mr Proila chuckled.

Molly had heard about cockerel fighting. She knew it was illegal. Before she'd owned the gold coin she would have found even the idea of it horrific. But today she felt differently. Now bad things, evil things, fascinated her. She smiled in anticipation.

'Good. Glad to meet someone who has the same tastes as me!' laughed Mr Proila, clocking Molly's reaction.

Suddenly the birds flew at each other, pecking and clawing, shrieking and crowing.

It was a vicious spectacle, but the crazed audience loved it. They took great pleasure from seeing the poor dumb roosters forced to fight. They cheered the cockerel they had bet on, and jeered whenever a bird showed signs of weakness.

To Molly's delight, it looked as though the cockerel with the black ribbon was winning. The other one was bleeding and its movements were slow. Her cockerel made one final lunge for its opponent.

'YES!' Molly shouted, punching the air, her eyes glinting cruelly. The man with the orange flag waved it above his head and the two cage-keepers stepped forward to retrieve the birds.

The losing cockerel looked half dead. The black-ribboned bird, still fired up with adrenalin and aggression, was difficult to catch.

'You win!' laughed Mr Proila.

'I know!' Molly laughed back. 'Is there another fight? Let's bet again.'

Mr Proila watched Molly. He liked this Moon girl and had a very good feeling about her. He felt sure they would work well together.

'Where did you get that?' he asked.

Molly hadn't even realized that she'd been gripping her gold coin. She saw his interest had been stirred. 'Oh, in Ecuador. A woman gave it to me. It's just an old coin. It's a bit of old rubbish really.'

'Doesn't look like rubbish to me,' Mr Proila said. He couldn't have the wool pulled over his eyes so easily. 'It looks like solid gold.'

'You know, Mr Proila, I'm tired,' Molly said, putting the coin away and changing the subject abruptly. 'Do you mind if we go? This has been a brilliant evening, but I've got to hit the sack.'

Mr Proila nodded.

As they moved through the crowd, Molly felt sure she saw fear in some people's faces when they saw Mr Proila. He led Molly towards a door at one side of the room where more bouncers stood guard. 'We'll have a drink before we leave,' he announced.

Not wanting a scene, and curious to see more, Molly nodded. Beyond the door was a room dimly lit with plum-coloured light shades. At the end of the room was a bar.

The bartender was pouring a drink for a man who stood with his back to the door.

The man was speaking loudly. His face and lips were visible in the reflection of the mirror behind the bar.

'Did you see him out there?' he was saying (though of course Molly didn't understand him at all). 'Winning again. The fights are rigged. He must bribe people to lose.'

The barkeeper raised his eyebrows to warn the customer that Mr Proila had arrived, but the man was too drunk to notice.

'That's how Proila got so rich,' the man slurred. 'By cheating. Cheating and conning. Tokyo was an easy-going place till he came along. My cousin runs a grocery store. Proila sends his heavies along every week. My cousin has to pay them not to burn his shop down.' He took a slug of his drink. 'The guy's a monster. He's not even Japanese. What hole of a place did he climb out of?'

Mr Proila watched the drunken man's lips in the mirror behind the bar. A sneer spread over Mr Proila's hard face. Then he strode towards the bar and hopped up on to a barstool.

The drunken man turned and suddenly saw who was next to him. 'Ergh . . . argh . . . Mr Proila!'

'Been in this town long? Maybe you speak English. Speak English so my young friend can understand.'

Mr Proila picked up a cocktail swizzler and began inspecting it, his stumpy half-finger twitching. 'So?'

The man nodded his head dumbly. 'Yeah, m-my . . . my grandfather born here, my father too, and so was I.

My family's been in Tokyo for hundreds of years.'

'Well, I wasn't born here,' Mr Proila replied, his voice icy. In a completely different tone he said to the bartender, 'Gimme my usual.'

The bartender nodded, picked up the silver cocktail shaker and began preparing the drink.

Mr Proila went on in a matter-of-fact voice. 'I wasn't born here, but, even so, this town is mine. Tomorrow, you are going to get out of my town. For good.' The man's mouth dropped open. 'If you delay for even a day . . .' Mr Proila insisted, watching the barman shake his drink, 'things will get very ugly for you.'

'B-but, Mr Proila, I didn't mean what I said. It was the drink talking. I got family here.'

The bartender passed Mr Proila his drink. He took a sip. 'I said, get out.'

The man practically tripped over his own legs as he turned. Miserable and terrified, he stumbled from the bar.

He brushed past Molly. She saw the fear in his face, but felt no compassion for him. She was impressed that a man as small as Mr Proila could be so feared. She stepped up to the bar and sat on the stool beside him.

'Do you have concentrated orange squash on the rocks? With a twist of Tabasco?' she asked the barman.

Mr Proila laughed. He translated Molly's request for the bartender. Then he lit one of his huge cigars.

'So . . .' he began, smoke puffing out of him as though his heart was on fire. 'So you want to work with me?'

Molly took a sip of her drink. 'It depends.' She eyed

Mr Proila's hand, with its missing finger, and wondered whether she ought to hypnotize him now. It would make everything much easier, yet it would also make things too easy. She knew she could get what she wanted from Mr Proila without hypnotizing him, and that would make her achievement all the more satisfying. Besides, hypnotized, Mr Proila wouldn't behave harshly towards her, and she wanted to get the worst of him. She wanted his insults; she wanted to counter his rude comments. She wanted to hit back and show him that she could match his darkness. If she hypnotized him, all the sport would be gone.

'Whether or not I work with you depends on what kind of deal you are prepared to give me,' she said.

Mr Proila grimaced. Molly didn't give him a chance to reply.

'I want a good apartment up front, all expenses paid. And cash up front too. Let's say five hundred thousand pounds worth of yen. As soon as I start performing, I want half of all profits. And I want to see your accounts so I know you're being fair. If I make you three million pounds of profit within a month, then my percentage goes up to seventy-five per cent. I'm not going to sign myself away like the boys did, Mr Proila. That would be stupid of me. I'd rather make it alone than do that.' Molly leaned towards Mr Proila. 'And believe me, Mr Proila, I really do have what it takes to make it alone.'

Mr Proila couldn't help admiring Molly's chutzpah. 'Oh yes? Then why do you need me at all?'

'Because of course it will be less effort for me if you are

my manager. And that is why you are getting half of the money I make.'

Mr Proila nodded. 'You're a piece of work, ain't ya?' He stirred his cocktail and took a sip. 'An' I like that. But if you do manage the three million profit in a month, it's fairer if we split it seventy–thirty. I'll deserve that for the things I'm gonna do to put you on the map. You should give me that extra five per cent.'

'What for? Protection money?' Molly said. 'You think I'm scared of you, Mr Proila?'

Mr Proila studied the young girl beside him. He had never come across a child so calculating, so ambitious, so fearless and so heartless. He liked her. If her talent was as truly special as the audience in the Tokyo Dome had thought, she was a genius product that was going to make him a fortune.

'So you're not afraid of me. You're hard as nails. No, Miss Moon, the extra five per cent isn't protection money, it's just for goodwill.'

Molly nodded. 'I see.' She slipped her hand into her pocket and stroked her coin. She didn't care what this silly little man was saying to her. He was as scary to her as a snake without venom. With one zap of her hypnotic eyes she could get him to do whatever she wanted any time she pleased. In the grand scheme of things the five per cent he wanted would be irrelevant. Anyway, eventually she'd send him packing. Mr Proila had no idea what lay ahead, she thought. Once she had no more use for him, she'd probably hypnotize him so that he ended up playing the penny whistle on the streets.

'OK,' Molly said. 'When I hit the big time, seventy per cent for me, thirty for you.'

Mr Proila offered his hand to Molly. 'Sounds like a deal.'

They shook hands. Then Molly raised her glass. 'Here's to me!'

Chapter Fifteen

When Rocky arrived in Tokyo, the others were still out at the concert. Miss Shonyo let him in.

He now sat on one of the pea beanbags, having a cup of tea with the old grandmother. Sobo had taken an immediate liking to her dark, good-looking guest.

When Rocky mentioned Molly's name, the old woman's expression grew stormy. She tutted and clicked her tongue. She shook her head at Rocky with such concern that Rocky wondered whether Molly was in hospital or, worse still, dead.

'Molly OK?' Rocky asked.

'Molly blam, blam, blam,' replied the grandmother, miming playing a guitar. Then she shook her head again.

Rocky frowned. Molly was definitely in trouble of some sort.

Suddenly the apartment door burst open and Petula

came running in, skidding across the floor to take a flying leap into Rocky's lap. She licked his face enthusiastically.

'Rocky, you're here!' Gerry rushed in and jumped on to Rocky as well. 'Isn't Tokyo cool? Meet Chokichi and Toka and Hiroyuki. You're going to really like them!'

Rocky smiled at the three brothers and stood up. 'Thanks for having me to stay,' he said. He tried to judge the Japanese boys. Were they the reason Molly was in trouble? Rocky had met a few hypnotists. So, suspicious of the boys, he was on his guard.

'Where's Molly? And how is she? Is she OK, Gerry?'

'She's very good at music,' Gerry replied. 'She's really got into her music.'

Rocky thought that this was an odd response, but before he could say anything, 'She very well,' Hiroyuki elaborated. 'She'll be back later, and you'll see. You're lucky to have her as a friend, Rocky. She's a genius.'

A genius? Surely Molly hadn't told these boys whom she hardly knew about her hypnotic powers!

'In what way?' he asked.

'In what way?' Chokichi laughed. 'In her musical way, of course. Wow, can she play guitar! Even with a lifetime's practice I couldn't hope to play that well.'

'Her harmonica's amazin' too,' Gerry agreed.

Rocky must have looked puzzled because Gerry asked, 'You do know that, don't you?'

'Of course I do,' Rocky lied, realizing that for now this might be the best strategy to help him get to the bottom of whatever was going on. 'It's just . . . she said

110

she was taking a break from her music.'

'Never!' Hiroyuki exclaimed. 'Molly must never stop.'

Rocky went over to Gerry, who was standing by the window looking glum. 'What's the matter, Gerry?'

'Oh, I'm cross because Mr Proila, the band's manager, told me that fish dealers in Tokyo market are selling bluefin tuna. They are very special rare fish. I hate those people. How come some people don't care about saving the beautiful things in our world?'

Rocky squeezed his shoulder. 'It's difficult when you care a lot about something like that but can't do anything about it because you're a kid.'

'Yes. I'm sick of watching adults messing things up.'

'Well, when you're older you can be a good adult and fix things.'

Gerry folded his arms. 'Yeah? That's a long time to wait though.'

Soon everyone decided to go to bed. Rocky was taken up to Toka's room, where there was another spare mattress. Gerry got into his bed with his clothes still on and yawned. He lay down and rolled over.

'By the way, Rocky,' he said, his eyes fluttering as he was already half asleep, 'Molly is a bit different. She reminds me of a mouse fed on sugar lumps. She's gone a little bit crazy.'

Before Rocky could ask any more, Gerry fell asleep. Rocky put on his headphones, opened his computer and began watching a film. He'd catch Molly when she came in.

When Molly got back to the apartment, the main living room was dark except for the lights of Tokyo that filtered in through the blinds. Molly sat down on the sofa and pulled out her coin.

Its power was incredible. It was like some fairy godmother, her powerful friend, with concern for Molly's success at its heart. She thought of how Petula and the old woman had attempted to steal it and she gritted her teeth with hatred.

'How did that old bat know about your power?' she whispered to the coin. 'Will she tell the boys? Would they believe her? No, they love me now. They'll just think she's a nutty old lady. And what about Petula? I suppose she sensed you. I'll have to keep you always close to me now. Don't worry. I'll look after you properly from now on.'

As she whispered she noticed that something was flickering on the balcony, just as it had the night before. There was definitely a man there. She immediately went to investigate. She squinted out but there was nothing there now. Could it have been just the city lights against the glass? She slid open the glass and stepped out.

Molly peered over the railing. No one was there. Molly frowned. Perhaps her tired eyes were playing tricks on her.

Back inside, she locked the sliding door, puzzled. 'It's too high,' she mumbled. 'Fourteenth floor. No one could climb up here.'

After changing into silk pyjamas, Molly got into bed.

She felt excited. Tucking the coin into her pyjama pocket, she shut her eyes and pictured her marvellous future. She imagined the awards she would receive. The Emmys and the Grammys, the Mercury and the BRITs. Imagining the platinum sales that her CDs would achieve, Molly went to sleep smiling.

At three thirty in the morning, Petula was woken by Gerry's flashing alarm clock. Gerry was quietly getting out of bed, taking care not to wake Toka, or Rocky, who had nodded off in front of his computer. Petula noticed that Gerry was fully dressed. Was he running away?

Gerry picked up his shoes and jacket and a small camera that stood on the chest of drawers. He sneaked out of his room and tiptoed down the stairs. Petula followed him. As he unlatched the apartment door and opened it, she slipped past his legs to the lobby outside.

'OK, Petula,' Gerry whispered. 'You can come with me.'

Instead of using the apartment lift, Gerry took the stairs. At the bottom he hid until the apartment-block doorman disappeared to his room and then took the opportunity to dash across the lobby.

The city was dark except for street lamps and a few lights in buildings. Gerry kept to the shadows. He didn't wanted to be spotted.

After a while he paused in front of a food shop beside a life-sized plastic model of a Samurai warrior that was advertising a brand of wasabi mustard. Here a street light cast a beam down and Gerry took a map from his pocket and opened it. A shadow suddenly blocked the light. Startled, he looked up. It was Rocky.

'What are you up to, Gerry?'

Gerry looked cross. 'Don't try to stop me, Rocky. I'm on a mission.'

'A mission?'

'Yes.'

'To do what?'

'You'll see. You can come if you like,' Gerry said cagily.

'Has this got anything to do with Molly?' Rocky asked.

'No. It's to do with sorting a mess out. 'Someone's got to do it. Are you coming?'

Rocky knew better than to demand an explanation from Gerry now.

'OK. Sounds exciting.'

Gerry and Petula resumed their journey with Rocky. Petula trotted in between the two boys, wondering what they were up to. Soon she noticed a smell of fish. As they walked, the fish smell got stronger and stronger and stronger until they arrived at a dead end. Lorries and trucks drove in and out of an entrance to a huge warehouse. People came and went on foot too. The place was humming, even though it was the middle of the night. Gerry strode towards it with the intention of a hunter. Among the hubbub, he, Rocky and Petula entered unobstructed.

Inside, men and women in white overalls were hard at work directing forklift trucks as they moved great frozen objects on to refrigerated lorries. It was like being inside a giant freezer. Cold air billowed from the ceiling, and icy jets hissed out from the walls. Lying in lines on the well-scrubbed, concrete floors, in crates or as big icy lumps, were chunks of fish, cut up and frozen. This, Petula realized, was a massive fish market. The chilly concrete hurt her feet. She didn't know it, but the sign above read: 'The Tsukiji Fish Market'.

'I think I can guess what you're up to,' Rocky said.

Gerry picked Petula up. 'This is the biggest fish market in the world, Rocky. The Japanese eat more fish per person than anybody else.'

Rocky had a feeling that Gerry might be intending to cause trouble, though he wondered how much trouble a boy of eight could cause in a huge fish market.

'You get every kind of fish 'ere. I looked it up,' Gerry went on. 'It's brought in by fishermen and then passed on to dealers who sell it to restaurants or to shops. Come on – let's take a look.'

Rocky and Petula followed Gerry into the labyrinthine warehouse. Petula counted the different types of fish smells as she went. Sardines, sprats, salmon, plaice, sole, swordfish. Herring and mackerel. It was four in the morning, and there were lots of business deals being done.

Gerry looked only at big fish before moving on. Rocky guessed what he was looking for. Finally they came to a grandstand at the end of the warehouse. Quite a few people were collecting there, preparing to buy.

Gerry picked Petula up again and, indicating that

Rocky should follow him, he stepped behind a tower of blue plastic boxes so they couldn't be seen.

'Hunting bluefin tuna is almost as bad as hunting whales, Rocky,' he whispered. 'I'm going to find the people who are selling it and take photos of them, and I'm going to tell them to stop it.' He fingered the camera that hung round his neck. 'The people who buy it are just as bad! Wait till you meet Mr Proila, Rocky. He's the nastiest bloke in the world. He eats bluefin tuna.'

'Does he have power over Molly?' Rocky asked.

'I don't know. Like I said last night, she's gone a bit crazy.'

Rocky nodded and was then distracted by the people in front of him. 'They look suspicious,' he couldn't help suggesting. He was catching the spirit of Gerry's mission. Part of him thought it was mad to take on a bunch of fish dealers, yet part of him couldn't resist. So when Gerry darted forward and hid behind another stack of pallets, even closer to the crowd, Rocky followed him. They noticed that some people were going through a plastic door beside the grandstand. 'We need to get in there,' mouthed Gerry, pointing.

The problem was a guard who was standing beside the door. Gerry took a calculated risk. Using a nearby broom, he used it to push a nearby pile of crates off balance. When the crates came clattering down, the guard on the door went to investigate. Gerry and Rocky ducked through the door and found themselves in another icy chamber.

Quickly they dived behind a forklift truck. Catching

their breath, they looked around. More people came in, each one looking furtively about. Rocky saw that Gerry was right. Some sort of underhand business was going on in this room, and he agreed that if it was bluefin dealing then it had to be stopped.

An elderly man in a dark blue overall and black rubber boots stepped up on to a platform and towards a lectern. He seemed to be the person everyone was waiting for, because a hush fell when they saw him. He put on a pair of spectacles and took a small hammer out of his pocket. Behind him, there were some large objects under black plastic covers. A woman stepped up and, with a dramatic flourish, stripped the black canopies off them. Huge slabs of meat were revealed. Gerry and Rocky realized instantly that it was whale meat.

Gerry was suddenly frightened. His eyes flitted about the room. This was far more serious than killing bluefin tuna. Whales were the greatest creatures of the ocean. It was completely horrific to kill and eat whales. He put his camera up to his eye and nervously began to take pictures.

Bidding began and soon became heated. As the auction went on, Gerry became more and more furious. He felt like running on to the dais and shouting a stream of abuse at everyone there, but his more sensible side held him back.

'We need to find out who's hunting the whales,' he said quietly to Rocky.

Rocky, who could hardly believe what they were witnessing, nodded.

They made a beeline for the door through which more whale meat was being carried. They slipped through easily because all eyes were on the frenzied auction on the stage.

Outside was an empty street where a lorry was parked with its rear doors open. Inside the lorry were a few sheets of black plastic identical to those covering the whale meat inside. Gerry clutched Petula tight and the boys ran across the yard and scrambled into the back of the lorry.

'They must bring the meat here in this truck,' Gerry said. Suddenly, there was a juddering and rattling. The truck's doors closed. Gerry, Rocky and Petula were plunged into darkness.

'How did that happen?'

'Don't worry,' Gerry whispered. 'They'll drive back to wherever they caught the whales, then they'll open the back to load more inside and we'll sort them out.'

Rocky wasn't so confident, but he said nothing. There was a rumble as the engine started.

'Jeepers, we're off!' Gerry exclaimed.

Chapter Sixteen

Molly felt for her coin. It was still safely tucked into her pyjama pocket, nestled there like an egg being incubated. She opened her eyes and blinked as a shaft of morning sun cut across her face. Sitting up in bed she took the coin out and stroked it. It made her feel fantastic.

She couldn't think what had possessed her when she'd called Rocky the other day. Had he arrived in Tokyo? she wondered. She must make sure she played him some music to stop him interfering.

Molly had no need of friends now. What could friendship offer her when she had the coin? All that she wanted was for everyone, from presidents to princesses, from film stars to the ordinary person on the street, to adore her. She wanted to be rich and powerful. She wanted to be able to go anywhere, have access to the best of everything – from palaces to private islands. There was nothing wrong with this, she thought. After all, she was Molly Moon, the world's best hypnotist, best time stopper, best time traveller, best mind reader, best morpher and now the best musician.

She knew she would master every instrument she tried. It was so easy! Eye hypnotism required far more effort than musical hypnotism. And time travelling felt irrelevant now; Molly felt no need to travel to another time – there was so much to see and do, and above all have, in this time. All her old talents felt too much like hard work now.

Hiroyuki and Chokichi were eating their breakfast. As Molly approached, the boys looked up and smiled at her, infatuated, still smitten by her performance the night before. A maid came out of the kitchen and curtsied to Molly, saying something in Japanese.

'She's asking what you'd like for breakfast,' Hiroyuki explained.

Molly took a look at the boys' tofu and cold fish. She didn't fancy that. Before she had owned the coin, she would have asked politely for ketchup sandwiches and concentrated orange squash, but, today, the mere idea of this food made her feel sick.

'Just coffee and toast,' she told the maid.

Hiroyuki translated, adding a please.

'You were brilliant last night. Everyone who saw you was blown away. Oh, and Rocky arrived. He's still asleep upstairs.'

Molly nodded. She would have a few hours before he

woke up as he would definitely be jet-lagged. Hiroyuki pointed to some Japanese newspapers on the table. Two had Molly's picture at the bottom of the front page.

'Look at that! They write about you in detail on page four,' said Chokichi.

Molly shrugged. She'd be getting the whole front page soon. 'What's Mr Proila's number?' she asked.

Hiroyuki and Chokichi opened their eyes wide. 'Man, you're so cool!' Hiroyuki said. 'You're not even fazed by being famous.'

'I've been expecting it,' said Molly. 'And this is nothing.'

'Wow!' Chokichi said.

'Mr Proila's number?' Molly asked again.

An hour later Molly was sitting in Mr Proila's apartment on the top floor of the Pea-pod Building.

The place had a safari theme to it. The floors were covered with zebra skins, and beside the main door was an umbrella container made from a hollowed-out elephant's foot. Dead animal heads – tigers, cheetahs, rhinos and even a hippo's – were arranged on the wall. The sofas and armchairs were blood-red velvet, some with the skins of more dead animals flung over them.

The low tables in the sitting area were black lacquer, shiny as polished glass. They were covered with a collection of little statuettes and ornaments, all of the same man in an old-fashioned army uniform. Molly sat down on the sofa and looked at them. The man wore high boots and breeches and a smart army uniform with a cape. None of the statuettes were more than forty centimetres high. Molly picked one up. She was turning it over in her hand when Mr Proila came in.

'Ah,' he said, clapping his little hands together, 'I see you've found my collection of Napoleons. I admire Napoleon. He was short, but he didn't let his height prevent him from being great, a great general of France. He died in 1821. He conquered Italy, Spain and other European countries and would have conquered Russia too if it had not been for the ice and cold conditions. World dominance was what he was after. I wonder why?'

He looked at Molly as though this question was also applicable to her. Molly wasn't sure what he was getting at. She decided to exercise her mind-reading muscles again.

She summoned a bubble above Mr Proila's head. Oddly it took a little extra effort today. When finally the bubble came, and she got her secret insight into Mr Proila's head, the pictures were faint and Molly had to concentrate doubly hard. It was the coffee she'd drunk, Molly guessed. She should avoid coffee; it obviously didn't agree with her.

In the bubble, she saw camera flashes going off. She saw herself, signing autographs all around the world. Then suddenly the images became fuzzy again. Molly pressed her mind to make the pictures come back into focus. 'What are you thinking?' she asked Mr Proila.

'Oh, nothing much,' he said. 'I'm waiting for your

answer, that's all. Why do you think Napoleon wanted world power?'

Molly smiled. She let the bubble pop. Then she answered. 'Napoleon obviously knew how talented he was,' she said. 'He knew that he was far cleverer than everyone else and that he should be in charge.'

'Maybe he was just an egotistical control freak,' Mr Proila pointed out.

Molly paused. 'I'm going to take over the world,' she said.

Mr Proila laughed. 'I know you're ambitious,' he chuckled, lighting a fat cigar.

'Ambitious is an understatement,' said Molly. 'And, Mr Proila, I've got a lot of countries to cover so I want to start now. Today.' Without waiting for a reply, she went on. 'I need a TV interview this lunchtime, on a top Japanese show. Put the boys on with me. Let me play the guitar. That'll turn the viewers on to me. Say I'm playing a free concert tonight at the Tokyo Dome. That'll get forty thousand hooked straight away.'

Mr Proila looked unconvinced. 'You must be joking.'

Molly shook her head. There was no time to dawdle. She decided to hypnotize Mr Proila. She switched her eyes on. But, strangely, they felt weak. Like a car with a flat battery, her hypnotic engine just wouldn't fire up. Finally, with enormous effort, her pupils dilated and she felt the purr of their power. It wasn't the faultless purr of just a few days before, but it would do. Making a mental note to practise a bit more hypnotism, Molly directed some of it into Mr Proila's eyes before what she had managed to muster spluttered and died.

He looked at her quizzically. 'Never noticed how green your eyes were before,' he said.

Molly had only a slight tingling fusion feeling. Mr Proila wasn't fully under her control at all. He was more charmed than hypnotized. Molly knew that weak hypnotism like this wouldn't stick for a long time, but it should be enough to persuade Mr Proila to give her her own way. So without wasting a moment she dived straight in: 'Come on, Proila. You know I can do it,' she coaxed.

Mr Proila rubbed his hands together. 'Good thinking,' he said, now mesmerized by Molly's idea. 'I'll get on it right away: an interview and the Tokyo Dome tonight.'

Molly smiled. 'You've got it, Mr Proila.'

By the time Molly had finished playing guitar on *Tokyo Talking*, Japan's top-rating TV show, the interviewer was totally besotted with her, and of course his huge audience was mesmerized by her too.

Molly felt fantastic.

Mr Proila sat in his office waiting for Miss Sny's Skype call to report on Molly's performance. When his assistant's face appeared on the screen, she was glowing. He read her lips. Demand had been so high that the Tokyo Dome ticket office had run out of tickets.

'OK, Sny. Make sure that the CD she records has a good picture of her. That'll be difficult. She's got a kinda ratty look.' A twisted smile contorted his face. The tills were going to be ringing their bells tonight, he thought. They'd be popping their cash drawers open and shut at the speed of a hummingbird's wings.

Chapter Seventeen

Many miles away, Gerry, Rocky and Petula were asleep in the back of the cold, smelly fish truck. They'd been stuck there in the dark, putrid space for seven hours. Their journey had been terrible and eventually they'd all dozed off. And the boys had wondered again and again how they had become trapped inside the lorry.

Eventually they were woken by it stopping.

Gerry and Rocky jumped up and began banging on the door.

'Help! Let us OUT!'

They pushed and kicked against the door, but it stayed sealed. Gerry sat on a plastic crate and put his head in his hands.

'What have I done?' he sobbed. 'This is like a coffin! We might die in 'ere and maybe no one will even know.'

He let out a frightened wail. 'Maybe they only use this truck once a week, or once a month. I'm so stupid. Just to find out who's being killing whales we're going to die.' Then he added bitterly, 'An' Molly won't bother lookin' for us. She probably 'asn't even noticed we're gone. Or if she has she's glad. What's 'appened to her, Rocky?'

Petula recognized Molly's name and guessed what Gerry was crying about. She hopped on to his knees to comfort him. Rocky put a hand on Gerry's shoulder.

'From what you've told me, she's in trouble, Gerry. More trouble than us. It sounds as though she's under the control of something. We'll get out of here, whereas Molly might be trapped forever.' Rocky wasn't sure they'd get out, but he wanted to make Gerry feel better.

'You really think so?'

Rocky nodded. 'I wish I'd got hold of Lucy and Primo before I left. I set off in such a rush that nobody knows where I've gone.'

'But we'll be out soon and you can call them then.'

'Hmm.' Rocky nodded and smiled as brightly as he could.

Suddenly a loud *CLUNK CLUNK* jolted the truck.

Gerry and Rocky leaped up and began to bang their fists on the doors again.

'HELP! HELP! WE'RE IN HERE! LET US OUT!'

There was a loud *KERKLUNK* of bolts being drawn, and then the metal doors opened a crack. Morning light poured in. The boys peeped out, squinting as their eyes adjusted to the brightness.

The truck had parked on a dock. In front of them was a small crane, and in the harbour water a small, rusty ship. Something huge glistened on its deck. It was a dead whale.

Chapter Eighteen

Molly was dressed in a green-and-red jumpsuit. Her hair had been dyed black and gelled and waxed into spikes. The high collar of her outfit was encrusted with large fake emeralds. The trousers were straight-legged. Her shoes were pointed green brogues.

She felt hip and cool. When she looked in the mirror she hardly recognized her made-up face, or her eyes that had been defined to look Egyptian. Tonight was the night. The Tokyo Dome stadium had been booked. And Molly planned to strike down every last person there with her music.

Molly picked up the ebony-forked guitar that Chokichi had lent her. She took the coin from her chest pocket and rubbed it. She winked at herself in the mirror. For a second she saw her reflection, as though she was a human-shaped coin, with variegated edges. The imaginary human-shaped coin in the mirror winked back at her. Molly knew that her mind was playing tricks on her because she was so excited.

There was a knock at the door. Miss Sny poked her head in and nodded respectfully. 'Excuse me, Miss Moon, you are due on the stage in three minutes.'

Cool as ice, Molly left her dressing room. She stepped through blue and white lights that lit her way to the microphone at the front of the stage and drank in the stadium's atmosphere. The applause from the hordes who had come to see her was tinglingly thrilling. Smiling, Molly hitched her guitar strap over her neck and took the arm of the guitar in her left hand.

Teasingly, Molly plucked her guitar's top string. A high note *tinged* out into the night. Molly, of course, had no idea what note it was. Nor did she care. She was already anticipating what a thousand notes from her guitar would do to this audience. She stepped up to the microphone.

'Good evening, ladies and gentlemen. Tonight, I'm going to play . . .' Molly raised her right arm high in the air . . . 'tonight, I'm going to play . . . ROCK 'N' ROLL.'

Molly brought her hand down hard and smacked the guitar's strings with her fingers. And the show was on the road.

She was brilliant. The audience went wild. Each sequence of perfectly executed notes was like a web spun by a master spider. The more the crowd listened, the more they became caught – trapped like flies. Molly drank up their appreciation. She had to agree, the music she was producing was genius.

And then she moved towards a drum kit that had been set up onstage. People could not believe it. This girl's skills were nothing short of miraculous.

Molly thrashed the drums, rolled them, beat the bass, tapped the snares and crashed the cymbals. And then she was finished.

The audience went crazy – so crazy that one of the usherettes who was selling Molly's CD worried that the building might collapse from all the excitement.

Molly was calm. Everything was going according to plan.

Gerry, Rocky and Petula saw the helicopter, a tiny dot in the sky, getting larger and larger. And now they shielded their eyes from the wind of its rotors as it landed on a cleared space on the dock.

After being found the friends had been forced to sit in the smelly truck to wait to meet the boss of the whale-meat operations. Time had passed to the horrid noise behind them of the chainsaw whining as it cut up the dead whale.

They were so exhausted when they were manhandled out of the truck that they felt nothing but numbness.

And then they saw Mr Proila. Dressed in a black suit and a long black coat, he stepped out of the helicopter. He began walking across the dock towards them.

'So,' he said, sneering at Gerry, 'I should have guessed that the little eco-warrior would try to spoil my fun.' He pulled Gerry's camera from his neck and lobbed it into the deep harbour water. 'You idiot brats!'

Gerry stared at the monster in front of him and, to his surprise, instead of saying something furious, he found himself saying, 'I feel sorry for you, Mr Proila. You don't have a single scrap of goodness in your heart, do you? I wonder why. Maybe it's because no one ever loved you when you were a little boy. That is really sad.'

Mr Proila hadn't expected this. He looked as though Gerry had slapped him. For a moment, he was speechless. Then he snapped, 'Put them in the cell. Let's give them a nice long time to think about their little let's-save-the-world moment and whether it was worth it.'

And without another word he turned on his Cuban heels.

Chapter Nineteen

If Gerry, Rocky and Petula had hoped that Molly was worried about them, they were wrong.

After the success of her TV appearance and her phenomenal live show, her old friends were as insignificant to her as caterpillars to a steamroller. Molly was intent only on her own forward movement. She didn't care what was flattened by her progress. And so, after coming off the stage at the Tokyo Dome, Molly ordered Miss Sny to put the next part of her plan into action.

'I'll need an Internet site for fans, and you have to arrange other venues. But not just in Japan . . .'

Molly wanted to conquer the world. She figured that it would take four tours around the world. Miss Sny, since she saw Molly as practically a goddess, and since she was also a brilliant organizer, was the perfect person to set these up.

Molly went back to the apartment tired and faintly satisfied. For a while she put up with Chokichi and Hiroyuki's fawning and flattery. Then she told them that she wanted to be alone. Eager to please her, they both went off to bed.

Molly sat on the sofa. She swung her legs up and put her arms behind her head. She lay there staring at the ceiling, from which hung a delicately balanced mobile. It bobbed about in the slight breeze that was coming through the apartment window.

And then Molly saw something on the balcony.

Someone was definitely out there again. A man. She was sure of it. She sat bolt upright. It was a man in a tweed suit. And he was wagging his finger at her like some sort of vision from a nightmare.

Panic and suspicion and fear shot through her. The person – whoever he was – was out to get her. She was sure of it.

The figure vanished. Molly dived for the lamp and switched it off to see outside better, then ran to the window. But the balcony was empty. For the first time it occurred to Molly that perhaps the person out there was a time traveller. The suspicion didn't last long. If they were, why would they only appear on the balcony? A time traveller who wanted her coin would be able to arrive in the room right beside her. There must be another explanation. She would tell Mr Proila the next day and have security tightened.

Just as Molly was relaxing again, she glanced behind

her and got another shock. On the back wall of the apartment, near the grandmother's shrine, hung scores of white-faced dolls. Each of the dolls only had one eye, and every single eye seemed to be staring straight at Molly.

She shuddered. 'You old witch!' she said, knowing that somewhere back there the old lady was watching her. Staring hatefully into the darkness under the stairs, Molly walked quickly past it and into her bedroom.

Molly woke to the sound of Miss Sny's fingernails tapping on her bedroom door.

'May I come in, Miss Moon?'

'Yes.'

Miss Sny slipped into the room as quickly as she knew how. She was carrying a breakfast tray with orange juice, croissants and coffee. Molly rolled over grumpily.

'You asked me to wake you at t-ten and b-bring you any feedback I've had,' Miss Sny simpered. 'Are you sure you don't want to wait till later?' I can always sit outside.'

'No, no . . .' Molly sat up, and took the tray. 'By the way,' she said, 'what are those weird one-eyed dolls hanging on the wall near the old bat's hideout?'

'Oh, oh, don't worry about those,' Miss Sny assured Molly. 'They are just *daruma*. The old lady has painted one eye on each doll to make a wish, and the idea is that when the wish is granted the other eye will be painted on too. She must want something very much!'

'Huh,' Molly grunted. 'She's mad. So, what have you got?'

Miss Sny perched herself on a stool and tapped on her laptop. 'It's extremely exciting,' she began. 'Our contacts in the West have been able to watch the footage we sent of you – and your fabulous show. . .' At this point Miss Sny sighed and paused to gaze adoringly at Molly.

'Get on with it,' Molly snapped.

'Oh yes, yes, well, the response has been amazing. They all want you: Moscow, Mumbai, Rome, Paris, Helsinki. Everywhere, Miss Moon, is desperate to have you perform.'

'Well, I can't possibly do all of them now,' Molly declared, taking a bite of her croissant. With her mouth full she grumbled, 'Warm my breakfast next time.'

Miss Sny looked crestfallen. 'Yes, Miss Moon.'

'I'll start with Moscow and Rome, then Berlin, Paris and Madrid, because I've never been to those cities. I'll tour the other places later.'

Miss Sny tapped her laptop. 'Are you sure you want to do a non-stop tour, Miss Moon? It will be very tiring.'

Molly held her knife in the air as she considered this.

'Yes,' she replied. 'I am. The sooner the whole world knows about me, the better. And we should leave on Monday.'

'That will mean the designers will have to be called in today. It's the weekend, so they . . . er . . . might not be able to—'

'Did they see the show?' Molly interrupted.

'Yes.'

'Then they'll come. On the trip I'll need hairdressers,

costume people, make-up.' Molly eyed Miss Sny and considered her. 'You can come. I'll need an assistant. I'll tell Mr Proila that if he wants me to be super-successful I'll need you. He's got other assistants who can do sign language and stuff, hasn't he?'

'Yes.'

'Well, he can use them while you're away.'

'Yes! Oh, thank you!' Miss Sny clapped her hands in blissful delight.

'But you're not coming if you do irritating things like that,' Molly said stonily.

Miss Sny immediately stopped and dropped her eyes subserviently. 'Sorry, Miss Moon.'

Chapter Twenty

olly stroked a white fox-fur hat and coat that had been ordered for her from the best furrier in Tokyo. She put them on and admired herself in the mirror.

'Better on me than on a fox,' she said to herself. 'Perfect for chilly Moscow.'

Her bedroom door opened quietly and Hiroyuki and Chokichi stood there.

'Are you off soon?' Chokichi asked sadly.

'Yes.'

The boys fidgeted. Molly ignored them.

'We're really worried,' Hiroyuki said. 'Yesterday Gerry and your friend Rocky left the apartment early and didn't come back. Do you think they went back to England? They didn't say goodbye.'

'No idea!' said Molly nonchalantly.

'Toka's been looking everywhere for them,' said Chokichi, shaking his head.

'Oh, don't worry about them. Really. They can take care of themselves.'

There was an awkward pause as Hiroyuki and Chokichi watched Molly zipping up her case.

'Toka wanted me to thank you,' Chokichi said.

'Oh yes?' Molly said, putting on a pair of furry ankle boots.

'Yes. Because of you, Mr Proila lost some of his interest in us. So Toka can leave the band. He hate being pop star so this is good for him and we are happy that he can follow his dream – join sumo wrestling school. Sobo is old friends with sumo wrestling master.'

'Sobo?' Molly asked distractedly.

'Our grandmother. We're very happy Toka is happy,' Hiroyuki said. 'Chokichi and I fine just the two of us. So thanks, Molly.'

Molly shrugged. The boys could become sewage workers for all she cared. She grabbed her case. 'Bye!'

Hiroyuki faltered for a moment, wondering where the warm Molly he had known had gone. But he was so infatuated by Molly's music that he soon smiled. He passed Molly a handful of tiny little origami animals. 'I made these for you.'

Molly nodded as she took them. 'Pretty!' she said.

On her way through the sitting room Molly saw the dark shape of the grandmother lurking in the shadows under the stairs. Molly winked at her and gave her a hard, cold smile.

Molly's whistle-stop tour began.

She flew by private jet to Moscow, arriving late at night. She stayed in a beautiful hotel on the Moskva River and woke to wonderful views of the capital – its grand old buildings topped with brilliant onion-shaped domes, some gold, others coloured and stripy like raspberry-ripple ice cream.

That day, Molly was driven around Moscow past impressive bridges and across ancient squares. Her day finished with a performance in the famous Bolshoi Theatre. The theatre was gold inside, with comfortable velvet seats and a wealthy audience. Molly thought this suited the first stop of her great tour perfectly.

As expected, her concert was a huge success – so much so that the next morning she had breakfast with the President of Russia. Then she was taken to the airport, where a private jet waited to fly her to Italy.

Gerry, Rocky and Petula sat in the bare room of a derelict fisherman's cottage. Rocky stared out of a tiny slit window at the open sea beyond, watching seagulls circling and diving. Gerry was making a mark on the grubby wall. It joined three other marks, showing that they were on their fourth day in the filthy cell. Rocky, of course, had told Gerry everything he knew about Molly – about her hypnotic eyes, her time-stopping and time-travelling skills, and even about her morphing. Gerry was amazed, and Rocky's stories were a good distraction from the cell. Gerry gave Petula a hug.

'I'm really sorry,' he apologized for the hundredth time. 'This is all my fault. I didn't think it through. I didn't think people could lock children up. Or dogs . . . and then forget about them.'

Petula nudged her nose under Gerry's chin. She knew things were bad. She wished she could talk and tell Gerry that everything would be all right. But inside she really was not so sure they would be. She knew that the men who had pushed her and the boys into this room were cruel and would do whatever Mr Proila ordered them to. Yet she knew she must hope. Without hope, this cell would be unbearable. She gave a small encouraging bark.

'I know, Petula,' Rocky said. 'I hate it too. But we have to look for signs that things will be OK. At least they're feeding us.'

'And,' Gerry added, 'they take away that bucket when it's got you-know-what in it. So, at least it don't smell in 'ere.'

Rocky sighed. 'Things could be worse. Just.'

Gerry pulled the small elephant-like origami animal that Hiroyuki had made him out of his pocket. 'I hope this little *baku* can eat up my bad dreams tonight,' he wished. 'It didn't work last night.'

Thousands of miles away, Molly was living the high life. As Gerry, Rocky and Petula ate soya beans, she dined on Beluga caviar and the finest foods. They knew nothing of her one-night stop in Rome or of the day she'd spent in Berlin and how crowds had gone berserk for her everywhere she played.

From Berlin, Molly jetted to France and that night performed at the Paris-Bercy Stadium. French traffic came to a halt all over the city as people stopped their cars to listen to Molly's concert, live on the radio.

Chapter Twenty-one

Molly sat in a comfortable armchair in her suite in the smartest hotel in Paris. She had her feet up and was reading a magazine called *Celebrity Society Whirl*. Faces of people at parties smiled out from the glossy pages. Molly gloated at the thought that soon every single one of them would be desperate to know her.

She slid and tumbled the gold coin along her fingers, thinking how well she'd perfected this movement. The coin seemed almost alive as it snaked its way between her knuckles. She sighed and looked out of the window.

Her suite overlooked the River Seine. Boats moved slowly up and down the water. She could see the famous cathedral of Notre Dame. She already loved Paris, with its beautiful buildings and promenades. She would certainly get herself an apartment here. She wanted one in New York too.

'I can get a secret apartment in Manhattan,' she whispered to the coin. 'Or one in the Statue of Liberty's head! Will that be good enough for you?' She laughed. 'You and me are a perfect pair. The best team ever! Oooh, it's SO EXCITING!'

Overwhelmed, Molly jumped up. With the coin between her finger and thumb, she whizzed round and round the room like a whirling dervish. 'I'm going to have everything I want! My own palaces, my own apartments, yachts, chalets, villas. I'll own islands and mountains and valleys! It's all going to be mine – MINE! And nothing – NOTHING – is going to stop me!'

Molly felt a bit dizzy. She sat down and held the gold coin to her chest. For a minute or two she sat there, panting and clutching it. Then she looked about her suspiciously.

She knew the coin had given her her power. There was no way she would have so many people under her influence without it.

Suddenly, as though a veil had been lifted from her eyes, Molly saw its worth. The coin was valuable beyond any price. Nothing in the whole world was as powerful. Molly saw that she owned something people would kill for. Kill *her* for.

Then again, she thought, how would anyone know she had it? They'd have to know how it worked. And who knew that? Miss Hunroe, the woman who'd owned it before, was no longer around. The Japanese grandmother was so senile Molly doubted she had worked it out. There was Mr Proila, of course. She'd been foolish enough to let him see the coin, but she doubted he guessed its power. Who else might have seen it without her knowing? There was a small chance that somebody somewhere out there knew about it. Perhaps Molly's sudden rise to international musical stardom was the sign they'd been waiting for. Perhaps they were coming to get her. Maybe the shadowy figure on the balcony in Tokyo had been after her coin!

Molly ran to the door and put a chair across it. She rushed to the hotel window and slammed it shut. But even as she did these things it occurred to her again that a time traveller could easily just pop up right beside her! She put her coin in her trouser pocket, then in her jacket pocket, then she hid it in her sock. Trying not to panic, she thought back, flicking through memories to see whether anyone had ever actually attempted to take her coin.

Petula, that smelly beast, had tried. The only human who came to mind was the Japanese grandmother. Molly remembered how she had found the old woman in her bedroom trying to steal it. How had she known about it? Were her senses simply more finely tuned than other people's?

Molly cast her mind back. The grandmother hadn't been able to actually take the coin. It had given her some sort of electric shock. It was as if the coin was loyal to Molly.

Then another thought struck her. Miss Hunroe's musical gift had not been remotely as powerful as Molly's. She had had her gaggle of obedient followers, but they were not completely devoted in the way that Molly's were. They weren't as bewitched.

It seemed that just as Molly had special talents with hypnosis, time stopping, time travelling, mind reading and morphing, she was also extra gifted with the coin.

She took it from her sock and spoke to it. 'Yes, I expect you're really glad I'm your mistress now, aren't you? You've been frustrated. You've wanted to channel your music, but the idiots you've been with haven't been able to make it happen. Luckily, I'm a genius.'

Molly felt much better. She decided that from now on she would be very careful not to flash the coin about. She'd keep her rooms locked and she'd keep bodyguards beside her if ever she went out. A time traveller arriving to snatch the coin was perhaps the worst problem she faced, but she reckoned the coin would repel them too.

Did the coin repel everyone? Molly simply had to know. She called room service.

'Send someone to collect my lunch tray,' she demanded rudely. Putting the phone down, she placed the gold coin on the tray that was to be collected.

Ten minutes later a waiter arrived.

Molly pointed at the tray. 'There,' she said.

The waiter came in to pick the tray up and spotted the coin. Naturally he reached down to pick it up.

'I sink zis is yo— AAAAAAAAAAAARRRGHH!'

Molly was pleased.

'Is zis some sort of joke-shop trick?' the man asked.

Molly shook her head. 'No,' she said. She had enjoyed

seeing the waiter's pain. 'Don't be silly. Pick it up and give it to me.'

The odd thing was that this time when the waiter touched the coin, nothing happened. Before Molly knew it, her precious coin was in his hands and, what was more, a sly look of interest had crossed his face.

'Give it to me, please,' Molly said.

Reluctantly the waiter passed her the coin.

'Thank you.' Molly tried not to snatch the coin back.

The waiter's eyes lingered on the coin. Molly slipped it into her pocket. That had been a mistake, she realized. But it had taught her that, if given permission by her, someone could take the coin. She vowed never to invite anyone to take it ever again.

She would hypnotize the waiter to wipe all memories of the coin from his brain.

'I think I've got something in my eye. Could you take a look?'

The man frowned, then nodded. He peered into Molly's eyes. 'Which one?'

Molly switched her eyes on.

'Which one?' the waiter asked again.

Molly stared at him. Oddly, nothing happened.

'Er, the right one,' Molly replied. As he studied her eye, Molly focused her mind as she had done countless times before, and, really concentrating, she summoned up all the hypnotic strength she could muster to send a pupil-locking stare into the waiter's eyes. This time it was Molly's turn to be shocked. Absolutely nothing happened. Molly was stunned.

'Hmm, actually it seems to have gone,' she said. Thinking quickly, she added, 'By the way, would you like me to play you something?'

The man looked delighted. 'Wow! Wow, yes, zat would be amazing, Miss Moon!'

Molly fetched her guitar. If her traditional mode of hypnotism didn't work, she'd have to use her musical hypnotism. She would mesmerize the waiter so completely that his desire for the coin would be overshadowed.

As she played, and watched the man's love-struck face, she was infuriated by how inconvenient it was that her hypnotism hadn't worked. She recalled the last time she'd used her eyes. It had been on Mr Proila. They had struggled to work then too, only strong enough to charm him. It was as if they had gradually been switching themselves off. Perhaps she was working too hard. Perhaps tiredness was to blame.

'My music will be all you remember about me,' she said. 'You can go now.'

When the waiter had left, Molly picked up her phone. 'I'm ready to go to Madrid now, Miss Sny. Arrange it.'

Gerry craned his neck to watch a plane flying over their small hovel. Seven nights had passed since they'd been caught, and with every day they had become more miserable.

'Look where we are, Petula! All shut up and forgotten about. It's like we're going to live in this 'orrible room for years and years and maybe we'll get out of 'ere when Rocky an' me are wrinkly old men. You'll be dead, cos dogs don't live as long as people. An' where will we bury you? Maybe we'll die 'ere too.' Gerry shivered. 'Wish they'd bring us another blanket.' He paused. 'I wonder where Molly is.'

Just as he said this, Gerry noticed a small mouse pop its head out of a tiny hole in the corner of the room.

'Pssst. Look, Rocky! Look, Petula!' he whispered.

They all sat very still and watched as the mouse disappeared again.

Rocky took the spoon that he had eaten his lunch with and knelt down. Nervously he began to scrape at the bottom of the wall.

To his delight, it crumbled. Gerry grabbed his spoon and the two of them set about frantically scraping and digging.

For the rest of the day the boys worked. By late that night they had made a hole big enough to squeeze through.

Petula followed them. They were all out.

To their left was the sea, to the right a road, and there, a little way along it, beside a bus stop, was a phone box. Luckily Gerry remembered Toka's phone number from when the Japanese boy had given it to him in Quito and Rocky had a few yen in his pocket.

'Toka, it's Gerry,' he blurted out.

'Gerry? Gerry, where are you? Are you OK?' came Toka's voice down the phone. 'I'm coming to get you.' BEEP BEEP BEEP went the telephone line, signalling

149

that the money was about to run out. 'Where are you?'

'Umm, I don't know, in a phone box.'

'Good, don't worry. I track number. I come to get you. Wait there. Don't worr—' The line went dead.

Gerry, Rocky and Petula hid behind some rocks where they could see the road but not be seen, and they waited. Every minute felt like ten for they were convinced that their escape would soon be discovered.

In the early hours of the morning a van drove quietly into the fishing village. It had a picture of a sumo wrestler with some Japanese writing on its side. Toka jumped out of it and Gerry, Rocky and Petula rushed to greet him. He helped them into the van. The old grandmother sat in the back seat. She hugged the boys and her eyes were brimming with tears. The driver, her old friend who was the master of the sumo academy, was at the wheel. He turned around and winked at Petula, then put his foot on the accelerator.

'Thank you. Thank you,' Gerry and Rocky said repeatedly. They'd never been so grateful in their lives.

Chapter Twenty-two

Mr Proila stood in his penthouse apartment in Tokyo, a glass in his hand. A large screen rose up out of a sideboard at the end of the room. He sat down in front of it and took a sip of vodka.

Moments later a black and white view of a sitting room came up on the screen. A view that was taken by a concealed camera in one corner of the ceiling.

Mr Proila watched the screen for a while. Nothing happened. He picked up the controls and began to stab at them. The film on the screen skipped forward. A girl now walked into the room very fast. Quickly she shut the door and leaned against it. Then she put her hand in the air as if celebrating something. It was Molly. Mr Proila jabbed at the controls and slowed the speed. Molly seemed to be talking to herself. Mr Proila read her lips.

151

'Good, good. You were brilliant . . . of course,' Molly was saying.

He watched as Molly admired herself in the mirror. 'Boring,' Mr Proila said. 'A prima donna loving herself.'

He fast-forwarded the film again. Molly took off her necklace and tweaked her hair. She took something from her pocket and stroked it for a bit, talking to herself all the while.

'Get yourself some company!' Mr Proila said. 'You'll go crazy if you talk to yourself so much.' He speeded ahead to the end of the film. 'OK, so that was Moscow. Let's see if Rome tells me any more about you.'

Again a hotel room appeared on the screen, this time filmed from a side angle. Molly came in, danced around a bit and then once again admired her jewellery. When Mr Proila slowed the film down, Molly was once again talking to a shiny locket or something.

'Between us we can do this,' she was saying. 'Working together, I am brilliant!'

'Now you're a split personality, are you?' Mr Proila said disgustedly. 'Stars, they're all the same – self-obsessed.'

He fast-forwarded to Paris. Everything was very similar – too similar. Mr Proila was beginning to find the whole business tedious. He was about to whizz to the end of the footage when something on the flickering screen caught his eye. He slowed the film right down.

Yet again Molly was talking to herself, but now Mr Proila saw that the shiny object between her fingers wasn't a piece of jewellery at all – it was a coin. A coin that he recognized. The coin she had had at the cockfight. Molly was rolling the coin through her knuckles, tossing it in the air and talking to it.

'OK,' she was saying, 'I'll do that. And what about tomorrow? Shall I do a long show?' Molly flipped the coin again and smacked it on to the back of her hand. 'Heads! Good. OK, I'll do it. Thank you for helping me. I adore you.' Mr Proila shrugged. So she was superstitious and used her coin to help her to decide what to do. He was about to press the 'off' button when he saw some extraordinary words come from Molly's mouth.

'With the music we make together,' she was saying, 'nothing can stop us. We'll control every single person on this planet. Except hairy hermits in mountain caves who don't listen to music, but who cares whether they are hypnotized or not!'

Mr Proila pressed pause and stared, stunned, at the screen. 'I don't believe it! It can't be true.' He rubbed his eyes. He rewound the tape and watched the footage again.

'. . . except hairy hermits in mountain caves who don't listen to music, but who cares whether they are hypnotized or not!'

Mr Proila watched as Molly carefully put the coin away in her pocket. He knew he was on to something.

Pouring himself another drink, he rewound the tape right back to the beginning. Now he meticulously began to study the film.

In Moscow he saw that Molly was stroking the coin. In Rome she congratulated the coin and Mr Proila watched as she tried the coin in different purses. 'No, that doesn't suit you,' she was saying. 'This one's too leathery. None of them is good enough for you, you perfect thing.'

In Paris Mr Proila now saw that she was talking to the coin again, not to herself. In Madrid, Mr Proila lip-read as Molly spoke to the coin more desperately.

'I mustn't let anyone find you,' she was saying. 'You're mine – mine alone. You know I'm your mistress, don't you? You'd electrocute anyone who touched you, wouldn't you? Like the Japanese granny. Stupid woman. She shouldn't have touched you. She deserved to be burned. She won't try to steal you again. You can only belong to someone else if I give you to them, or if I lose you, can't you? And I'll never do either of those things – so we're together forever and forever!' Molly hugged the coin to her cheek and shut her eyes.

Mr Proila's eyes widened as he watched. To start with, he kept saying, 'Weird, just weird!' He wondered whether the vodka was making him imagine things. But the more he watched, the more he found himself facing an undeniable truth. Molly believed that the coin she carried helped her make hypnotic music.

Now Mr Proila saw that Molly's behaviour was paranoid and nervous. She was sitting scared in her room, glancing this way and that as though expecting an invisible attack.

'That coin is getting to you, li'l girl,' Mr Proila chuckled.

'Looks as if you should let someone else look after it.' He switched the monitor off.

As the screen dropped back into its concealed home, he tipped the last of the vodka into his mouth.

'The question is, how do I get you to part with it?'

Chapter Twenty-three

A few days later a black jet landed in Tokyo airport. The sleek aircraft taxied off the runway to a special hangar, where Molly disembarked. A white Bentley awaited her. Molly climbed inside, with Miss Sny, and was whisked away.

Fans lined the road from the airport. Molly ignored them.

'So, Miss Sny. I expect sales of my CD have done well this week?'

'Oh yes, Miss Moon.'

'And my bank account is filling up even more?'

'Yes, it's b-burgeoning, Miss Moon.'

'Burgeoning? Why are you trying to use fancy words, Miss Sny? They don't suit you. You're not that clever. Burge-what-ing? What does that even mean?'

Miss Sny stuttered nervously. 'B-burgeoning – it

means overflowing with—'

'Burgeoning – yes, I like that word. It suits me down to the ground. I'll use it from now on.' Molly pointed a silver fingernail sharply at Miss Sny. 'But you, Miss Sny, are never to use that word again. Got that?'

'No, Miss Moon, I mean, yes, Miss Moon. I wouldn't dream of it.'

By the time Molly got back to the Pea-pod Building, she was very short-tempered. 'So annoying not to have my own place,' she grumbled as they stepped into the elevator. 'Find me a property, Sny. Suppose I'll have to talk to those Japanese twits again.'

'Er, oh. Sorry, sorry. I'm so sorry,' Miss Sny apologized. 'The boys are working late in the studio, Miss Moon, so they won't be there. But I hear that someone is waiting for you – a Mr Scarlet.'

Molly's eyebrows arched. 'Oh, him. I'll go up alone.'

'Yes, Miss Moon.'

When Molly stepped into the apartment, Rocky was looking out of the window at the glittering night view of Tokyo.

On hearing the door close, he turned. His face lit up. He rushed towards Molly and threw his arms around her, giving her a massive bear hug. Molly, cold as a marble pillar, made a face at the physical contact. Rocky didn't notice. Grinning, he drew away from her.

'Don't ever do that again,' Molly said crushingly.

'Things are not like they used to be. I . . . I am different.'

'I know, I know – you are brilliant!' Rocky exclaimed. 'Your music is genius! I can hardly believe it! My friend – my friend Molly – is world famous!'

Molly interrupted him. 'I'm not your friend any more. You can forget that idea, Rocky. You knew me once, that's all. I'm an independent person now and far superior to you.'

Rocky's face dropped. 'But . . . but, Molly, what are you saying? We're like brother and sister.'

Molly laughed. She had been prepared to play guitar to Rocky, but it was obviously unnecessary. He was already putty in her hands. 'No, Rocky. I don't have any family,' she said with fake sadness. 'Neither you nor Gerry nor Petula are family to me any more. I'm alone, and I like it this way.' Molly turned to the fridge. The idea of friendship made her feel queasy, and she didn't like the look on Rocky's face that seemed to be begging her to be friends with him again. On the wall behind him the one-eyed Japanese dolls stared at Molly. 'I can't believe those ugly things are still here,' she commented. 'Must get rid of them.'

'Where are Gerry and Petula?' Rocky asked, knowing full well that they were safe in the van with Sobo and the sumo master.

'Who knows?!' Molly answered. 'Who cares?!' she added, cracking open a can of mineral water.

Rocky observed her coolly. 'I know someone who knows,' he said. 'That person thinks there's something

158

weird going on with you, Molly.' He stepped up closer behind her.

When Molly turned around, Rocky was right behind her. He grabbed the collar on her dress and pulled her towards him. She was taken completely by surprise.

'Guess what, Molly, I am not under your power. What is more, I believe you are under the influence of someone or something else. Don't try to hypnotize me with your eyes. I'm too alert. You won't be able to.'

Molly looked stunned. She dropped her can of water and clamped her hands over her ears. 'You've come to hypnotize me, haven't you? With your voice. But I won't let you. Anyway you were never very good at it.'

Rocky pulled one of Molly's hands from her ear. 'I've come to help you get yourself out of whatever trap you're in. It's obvious to anyone who knows you that there's something weird going on . . . unless they're hypnotized by this music you play.'

He let her hand go. Molly reached into the pocket where she kept her mouth organ. Just a few notes were all that were needed. She'd once liked Rocky, she thought, but now she loathed him, for his interference, for his desire to spoil her future.

Before she could bring the instrument to her lips, Rocky gripped her wrist. He shook it till the harmonica clattered to the floor.

'Something's helping you play these instruments,' Rocky growled. 'It's not a person, as a person couldn't give you all this musical knowledge. It's something powerful. Sobo told me about a weird coin you carry in your pocket.'

'GET O—' Molly started to cry out.

Rocky pushed her backwards. At the same time, he reached for her jacket pocket.

Molly struggled and twisted and then she began laughing. 'This is going to be funny. You're going to get such a surprise!'

Rocky ignored her. His hand delved into the first pocket. Empty. And then into the one where the coin was. As soon as he touched it, he yelled and retracted his hand. In pain and shock, he let go of Molly.

Mr Proila sat in his apartment, watching all of this on his special screen. He'd heard from Miss Sny that Molly was returning to Tokyo, and so he had set up three concealed cameras in the boy band's apartment. Now he watched Molly leap away from the boy who had been her friend and retrieve her mouth organ. He saw the boy snapping earphones over his ears and then diving for Molly again. It was clear to Proila that the boy was in a weak position, for if Molly dislodged his earphones he would be vulnerable to her powerful music. When she dived for his head, he only just managed to dodge her. And then he fled.

Rocky ran as fast as he could out of the apartment, into the lift and out on to the street.

There was the wrestling school van, with the sumo

wrestler on the side. The back door opened and Gerry and Petula peered out.

'Not good?'

'No!'

Rocky jumped in, banged on the front wall of the van, and with a screech they were off.

Up in the apartment, Molly was furious. 'Let him see how far he gets! He's nothing. He's pathetic!'

Mr Proila strode in. 'Molly!' he gushed. 'I turned your music up loud and felt its power! You're incredible – you're a superstar.'

Molly ignored Mr Proila. She was too angry to listen to him.

'Oh, oh! It was superb,' Mr Proila enthused. 'I've never experienced anything like it. In fact –' his face crumpled with emotion – 'in fact, Molly, no art has ever moved me as much. Your music is phenomenal – I *felt* it.' He pressed his hand to his heart.

'Not now!' Molly snapped. 'Damn!' she spat. She slumped on to the sofa. Then she eyed Mr Proila suspiciously. 'You felt my music?'

'Yes! Yes. I turned it on loud. I felt its rhythm through the speakers. Its vibrations through the floor, through my feet. You are . . .' Mr Proila acted as adoringly as he could. 'You are a genius. An – an angel!' He looked at Molly's cross face. 'But you seem upset. Can I help?' he asked innocently.

Molly sighed. 'I wish you hadn't done that,' she said

disappointedly. 'I liked you so much more when you weren't besotted. Now you'll be just like all the rest. But,' she said slowly, considering him, 'you *can* do something for me. There was a boy here just now. I need to track him down. And then, maybe, I'll need to get rid of him. Can you do that for me?'

'Of course,' Mr Proila said agreeably. 'I'll see to it. I'll call security.'

'And by the way, Proila,' Molly added, not losing an opportunity to get what was hers, 'I want all the money that I've made so far put in my own bank account today.'

'It's there!' Mr Proila exclaimed. He paused. 'And, actually, I wonder whether I might suggest something for you? I would like to plan a tea ceremony for you, Molly. Not an ordinary tea – a Japanese ceremonial tea. Since experiencing your music,' Mr Proila went on, acting as though he was being as thoughtful as he possibly could, 'I've realized we must mark this stage of your brilliant career. I know how fine things appeal to you – things of quality and high artistic achievement – and I think a Japanese tea ceremony would satisfy your taste. Only those of the highest sensibilities can appreciate its subtlety and sophistication.'

Molly nodded. 'Yes, anything of great beauty helps me,' she agreed.

'Oh, I am so glad,' Mr Proila said, smiling. 'Remember, I am always at your service.' He bowed and walked backwards out of the apartment and into the lift. 'And I will find that boy for you. Do you have a preference for how you'd like him disposed of?'

'I'll choose the method when you've caught him,' Molly declared. 'And I'll have that Japanese tea this afternoon.' She muttered to herself, 'I'll probably be so highly irritated by then that I'll need some high culture to soothe me.'

'Certainly, certainly,' said Mr Proila, popping out of the lift and bowing again.

'And, Mr Proila, you look like some sort of bobbing car ornament when you do that. Cut it out. It doesn't suit you.'

Mr Proila backed into the lift and straightened up. The door slid shut.

Inside it a look of sly malevolence darkened Mr Proila's face. He jabbed at the lift button. 'Gotcha!'

Chapter Twenty-four

Sobo's old friend, the elderly sumo master, changed gear. Intent on the road and glancing repeatedly in his mirror to check they weren't being tailed, he drove as fast as he could.

'OK, it's OK,' Sobo assured Rocky, reaching into the back of the van and patting his arm with her papery-skinned hand.

Rocky nodded at her. He was still shaken from his encounter with Molly. She had been like a possessed person or a monster.

'What 'appened?' Gerry asked.

The van drove through night-time Tokyo to an old-fashioned district. It pulled up in front of a bamboo-roofed wooden building. A sign written in Japanese and English said: 'Ryogoku Sumo Stables'.

Gerry and Rocky jumped down from the van and helped the old lady into her wheelchair. With Petula trotting alongside, they pushed her up a vine-canopied path to a door. As soon as they were inside the school's simple whitewashed hall, they took off their shoes.

They made their way up a wide passage with big doors set at intervals up one side. Noises – slaps and grunts, the sound of shuffling and thudding – came from the rooms beyond. Through the glass panels in the doors the friends could see sumo students training.

Gerry stopped to peer into one room. Overweight Japanese boys wearing nothing but white loincloths sat along the edges, watching other boys who stood inside a square that was drawn on the floor. The boys in the square were standing with their legs apart, bent forward, facing each other as if about to fight. A man in a blue kimono, who was obviously their teacher, pointed a stick at them and shouted, 'Oih!'

The boys slapped their knees and dived at each other. For a moment they struggled, grabbing at each other's loincloths as they each attempted to knock the other over. Then one pushed his opponent out of the ring. The match was over. Gerry saw Toka in the classroom and signed to him that they would meet him back at his bedroom.

Toka's teacher, the sensei, had agreed to allow Toka to share his room with Gerry, Rocky and Petula. There was just enough space for three single beds. These were now rolled up. The paper shutters on the windows let in light from the street.

Rocky and Gerry were sitting cross-legged on the bamboo matting with Petula curled up beside them when Toka came in.

'So you didn't get coin,' he guessed.

'No, I couldn't,' Rocky said. 'I tried to, but touching it hurt like hell. And Molly was horrific.'

'What shall we do?' Toka asked, sitting down. 'We've tried your parents and Forest . . .'

'She's so cunning,' Rocky ruminated.

'So how long was the CD she sent them?' Gerry asked.

'Long enough to hypnotize them,' Toka answered.

'Do you really think they won't come out here, Rocky?'

'Not after she told them not to. Gerry, even if we beg Primo and Lucy to help us, they won't listen. She's brainwashed them. She brainwashes everyone. Her music is addictive. People listen to it once and get hooked and then they listen to it more. And each time they fall deeper and deeper under her musical spell. Even the police are her fans. It's really creepy.'

'Scary,' Gerry said, biting his lip.

'You got to look on bright side,' Toka pointed out. 'We lucky. No Molly Moon music here. So we grow strong. We prepare. We will fight. We will win fight. We get coin.' He paused. 'Sobo says the coin has evil *kami* in it – evil spirit. Sobo thinks we must destroy coin. But that difficult. Molly keep coin so close to her, and she surely keep bodyguards always with her, now that you shock her.'

'Maybe another opportunity will crop up,' Rocky said. 'There's got to be a way to get the coin. The trouble is, it's not exactly Molly we're dealing with here. It's a monster. The worst part is that Molly, our friend Molly, is locked up inside the monster. We have to help her.'

'Poor Molly,' Gerry gasped. 'You're right, Rocky. We've got to 'elp 'er escape.'

Chapter Twenty-five

Molly glanced at her watch. She was looking forward to the special tea ceremony. It was almost teatime now and, as she'd predicted, she was starting to find her surroundings tiresome and the people about her infuriating.

She had spent the last few hours looking at possible apartments to buy. None of them seemed good enough. She had ordered a new car and had some bluefin tuna sushi for lunch, and then she had opened boxes and boxes of new clothes and shoes. Now she was in a baggy green velvet jumpsuit with skeleton buttons and green satin sneakers. Round her neck she wore a gold chain with a green glass eyeball hanging from it.

'IS THE CAR READY?' she yelled to Miss Sny.

'Er, yes . . .' Miss Sny said, scurrying into the room. 'It's outside.'

'Good.'

The car drove swiftly through the city. Finally it pulled up in front of a very plain modern-looking building.

'What's this?' Molly demanded. 'Doesn't seem anything special. Thought we were coming to an amazing tea house.'

'Ah, yes, it looks ordinary on the outside,' Miss Sny agreed. 'But don't be fooled! The tea house and its wonderful gardens are inside the walls. W-w-would you like me to accompany you?'

'Certainly not. I want this experience to be as good as possible.'

Molly stepped out on to the pavement, and without so much as a backwards glance dismissed the driver by tapping on the top of the car.

One of Mr Proila's men opened the door to the private space beyond. Molly had never seen him before and she was again impressed at the number of bodyguards Mr Proila employed. The man bowed as he let her pass.

The sound of water was the first thing that Molly noticed when she stepped in. She found herself in a beautiful garden with ponds and waterfalls. There were pretty mossy areas and bamboo copses and a few small trees, each in the early stage of budding. In the middle of the ponds were strange upright stones. A white gravel path with gates led to a tiny, wooden building with a winged roof on the other side of the garden.

'That is tea house,' Mr Proila's man informed Molly. 'And that –' he pointed to a more substantial, old-fashioned building made of stone – 'that is ryokan. You go to ryokan, change for ceremony. Mr Proila wait in tea house.'

Molly nodded and set off towards it. On either side of the garden were tall windowless office buildings. This gave the impression that the garden was cradled and safe.

'Now, this is interesting,' Molly said to the coin. 'I was so irritated by everyone just now. But this place has made me feel better. It's charming.'

As Molly admired the ornate gables over the tea house's windows she imagined that this place was already hers. Mr Proila was now a dumb, totally dedicated fan. She knew he would give it to her.

At the entrance of the ryokan a skinny man in a black kimono bowed low. With outstretched hands and flat palms, he presented Molly with a pair of strange glove-like socks with buttons. 'These "*tabi*",' he said. He passed her some wooden-soled flip-flops. Molly smiled. She sat down and changed out of her green satin sneakers.

A small woman in a yellow kimono appeared to Molly's left. Also bowing, she held out a green kimono for Molly.

'Hmm – a coincidence,' Molly observed. 'My favourite colour. Where do I change?' Molly pointed at her own clothes and then at the green kimono. The woman nodded and curled her finger, indicating that Molly should follow her.

They made their way along a low-ceilinged passageway, Molly treading quite slowly in the traditional Japanese shoes. They passed through a sliding paper-panelled door and along a passageway with a tiny bathroom at the end.

Molly was left to change into the green kimono. She was careful to put her precious gold coin into its pocket, along with a handful of yen. Five minutes later, the woman returned and tied Molly into the kimono. She ushered her towards a stool and opened a pretty enamelled make-up box. Before long Molly looked like a traditional Japanese geisha girl, with whitened skin and rosebud lips. Black sticks in her hair completed the picture.

Molly shuffled to the ryokan's front door.

'When you get to tea house, sit on seat there,' the woman told her. 'Garden calm mind and senses.'

Molly walked back through the magical garden and sat on the seat. A minute later, Mr Proila came out. He put his hand to his mouth in delight when he saw Molly. She suspected that he had been waiting all afternoon for her to appear. He was also dressed in a kimono. His was black silk, with gold coins embroidered on its lapel.

'Nice outfit, Mr Proila,' she said.

'Thank you so much,' he said. 'And you, I must say, look enchanting. Now, Molly, the first thing you must do is cleanse yourself. This stone water basin is a *tsukubai*. You must take some of its water and rinse your mouth and then your hands. That is part of the ceremony.'

'I love it!' said Molly, and she did as he said. Then her host led her inside.

The interior of the tea house was a picture of simplicity. In an alcove facing the entrance was a scroll with Japanese writing on it. A simple flower arrangement stood below in a vase.

In the centre of the room, in a sunken square section in the floor, was a hearth where a charcoal fire burned. Beside the hearth were two cushions, one red and one black. A woman in a light blue kimono busied herself with a kettle.

'I like the pad,' Molly commented.

'I'm so glad you do,' Mr Proila gushed, bowing as he spoke. 'This building is three hundred years old. It has been frequented by Japanese notaries, noblemen and women and sophisticates since it was built.' He spread his small hand out. 'Please, Molly, be seated. You are in the place of honour.' He let Molly make herself comfortable on one of the cushions while he stood, and then he lowered himself on to the other like a duck on to an egg.

The woman in the blue kimono carefully laid out porcelain cups and saucers on a large tortoiseshell tray. Then she placed a small antique teapot, a gold whisk and linen cloths beside them. Mr Proila gazed at Molly. The woman took some powdered tea from a tea caddy and sprinkled it into the teapot. She added some hot water from the kettle and stirred it with the gold whisk.

'It is marvellous,' Mr Proila enthused. 'These things have been used for hundreds of years. That is why Miss Oko here uses them with such reverence.'

Mr Proila poured two tiny cups of tea and then put his hands together and shut his eyes, as though praying.

'Drink down in one,' he said, nodding solemnly.

Molly shrugged. She sipped at the tea. It was warm, with an orangey tang. As instructed, she drank the cupful in one. 'Best tea I've ever tasted. Well done, Mr Proila! For a little person, you've got a lot of style!'

Mr Proila leaned towards her. 'If you are fond of tea, perhaps the tea house could be yours.' He filled her cup again.

Molly nodded and smiled. 'That is what I was thinking,' she said. 'It will be one of my little treasures.' She knocked the second cup of tea back as easily as the first.

'They always say,' Mr Proila said, 'that three cups are for good luck. But you've probably had enough. I will pour my own.'

'No,' Molly said. 'Me first. Cour me another pup.'

'Certainly.'

Molly downed her third cup. When she looked up there were two Mr Proilas sitting before her. 'I didn't know you had a brother.'

'I do,' Mr Proila said. 'He's taller than me.'

'He doesn't seem it,' Molly said. 'And he talks at the same time as you.'

'Yes,' Mr Proila said. 'Is he talking as I'm talking? So rude!' he chuckled. 'How are you feeling, Molly?'

Molly's head swam. She felt wonderful. It was as if she was sitting in a magical grotto, for the ceiling seemed to shine, and she felt full of excitement and warmth. It was a sort of birthday feeling, but a thousand times as strong.

'Now I know why people have been drinking tea in

this tea house for hundreds of years. It's very special,' she said.

Mr Proila laughed. 'Yes, very special. And to make one's first experience here extra special, it is customary to give presents.'

'Oh! Lovely,' Molly gasped. 'I love presents! And I deserve lots too, seeing that I am so brilliant!'

'This one is for you!' Mr Proila passed Molly a red velvet box. When she opened it, she found a gold medallion with the words 'Thank you, Molly' engraved on the front. On the back was Japanese writing.

'That side says "Thank you, Molly" in Japanese,' Mr Proila said.

Molly thought how sweet Mr Proila looked, like a cuddly mascot. The coins embroidered on his lapels were amazing. They seemed to tumble down his chest like golden water.

'Thank you, Mr Proila!' Molly said. 'And, by the way, you must tell me where you got that kimono – it's great. I want one too.'

Molly hung the medallion around her neck. She smiled at Mr Proila.

He looked expectant. 'The tradition is that you give me a present too – it's for the good luck to work,' he explained.

Molly nodded. 'Yes, of course. The tradition. I love tradition – handed down from age to age . . . and luck is a good thing too.'

'Yes, you hand something to me, then the tradition is

174

passed on. Do you have any jewellery?'

Molly shook her head.

Mr Proila looked worried. 'For the luck to work, the present must be given.'

As Mr Proila spoke, Molly's heart started to beat faster. The joy and wonder of the room, and of her life as it was now to be, blissful and perfect like this forever, felt like it might shatter if she did not give Mr Proila a gift.

'Perhaps you have something in your pocket you could give me,' Mr Proila suggested kindly.

Molly felt inside her pockets. In one there were a few bits of paper with Japanese faces on them. 'Would you like these?' she said, offering the yen notes to him.

'The present has to be something more special,' coaxed Mr Proila. 'Perhaps in your other pocket?'

Molly felt about in her kimono. She pulled out a big heavy disc. It was the gold disc she'd been carrying about for . . . for what reason, Molly couldn't remember – for good luck, she supposed. She smiled and held it out to Mr Proila. 'Here, Mr Proila, take this. It's jewellery of some sort. Do you think it'll make the luck work for us both?'

Mr Proila put his hand out. 'Let me see. Perhaps it will.'

Molly watched as he took the disc. His eyes lit up as his fingers felt it, and then they shut and Mr Proila pressed the disc to his chest. Then he quickly put it in an inside pocket. When he next looked at Molly, his eyes were cold and mean and angry. He rolled up his kimono sleeves, revealing the tattooed snakes on his arms. He stood up, pushing the table roughly so that the cups and teapot clattered against each other and a few porcelain bowls fell to the floor and smashed. 'You stupid little girl,' he said.

'W-what are you doing?' Molly laughed. 'The cups have all broken! And I love the pictures on your arms.'

'I'm putting an end to you!' Mr Proila snapped. 'Fun time is over, Moon. You may think the world is perfect right now, but I assure you it isn't. When the drug that was in that tea I gave you wears off, the world is going to seem black. Black as grimy soot. But even then you'd better enjoy it, because tomorrow it's curtains for you. And I don't mean the stage kind. I mean the hello-death, goodbye-life curtains. I've had enough of you, Moon!'

Molly couldn't help laughing. 'Oh, you're so funny, Mr Proila! You look so sweet doing your Mr Bad Guy act!' She looked at the quiet woman in the blue kimono who was staring icily at her. 'And your sidekick is so cool!' Molly was brimming with pleasure. Nothing could stop the happy feeling inside her. She had no idea what was really happening.

The door opened and two muscly men came in.

'Take her to the cell,' Mr Proila ordered them.

The men approached Molly and carried her out of the tea room.

Molly began giggling hysterically. 'Oh, I'm really ticklish. Stop it!'

The big men carried Molly through the beautiful water-filled leafy garden, back to the ryokan.

'Ah, home sweet home,' she sighed as they took her down some stairs there. They deposited her in a tiny room with a small window. 'Oh, this is such a nice place! So calm and peaceful and simple!'

The guards gave her a look that she found enormously amusing. She burst out laughing. They left, locking the door behind them.

'Thank you!' Molly called after them. 'I love this place!' She took off her wooden shoes and lay back on the floor, gazing with appreciation about her. She admired the jagged cracks in the antique plaster on the walls and the stains on the ceiling that made such pretty patterns. The light outside filtered through the tiny barred window, that to her looked like the iron pillars of a miniature ancient portico.

'Ahh,' she hummed to herself. Then her eyes began to glaze over. She was exhausted. Content as a field mouse in its woven nest, Molly curled up and fell asleep.

Back in the tea room, Mr Proila was sitting with his feet up on the table. 'When the drug has worn off,' he said to his bodyguard, 'I'll have made up my mind what to do with her. Now, one of you – go to that instrument shop on Meida Dori Avenue in Ochanomizu. I've ordered a grand piano. Make sure it gets delivered to my apartment. And bring the violin, the electronic keyboard and the flute I've chosen here. The traffic's bad, so get on with it. I'll be in the retiring room on the top floor of the ryokan.'

*

Molly slept contentedly for about half an hour. She felt very strange, heavy-headed and bleary when she woke up. For a moment she didn't know where she was. Then she shook her head and remembered the pretty tea room and the sweet, peaceful . . .

Molly sat up. Was this the same room she'd gone to sleep in? The one with the pretty ceiling? In a flash Molly saw that it was but that it was nothing more than a crumbling cell. In the next second she remembered Mr Proila and the tea ceremony. Like a horrific beast rising up to greet her, the truth of how Mr Proila had tricked her and imprisoned her was overwhelmingly clear.

He had taken her coin, her precious coin – the one that she had loved – the coin that had helped her hypnotize the world! Molly shook. Beads of perspiration began to gather on her forehead. She felt hot, really hot, as though she might explode, and then, suddenly, she felt cold – cold as the stone floor beneath her. Her teeth began chattering.

Tears welled up in her eyes and ran down her face. She felt a horrible, lonely pain in her stomach, as though she had lost her closest friend. She knew the only thing that could make the pain stop was the coin. She bent over, clutching her stomach, rocking back and forth, moaning.

She thought of the coin now, in Mr Proila's possession. A jealousy, the likes of which she had never felt in her life, engulfed her, drowning her in its green fury.

'It's mine,' she hissed. 'MINE!'

She thought about the lovely music she'd made. How she wished she could hear even a note of it right now. But as she wished she caught sight of a tiny thought waving frantically to her from the corner of her mind. The thought suddenly shouted, 'HE'S GOING TO KILL YOU! GET OUT OF HERE!'

Molly looked at the tiny barred window and then at the heavy cell door with its small viewing pane. Suddenly she was petrified. Adrenalin began pumping through her veins, making her focus. She wanted her coin back. But she had to forget that for now. Right now she had to escape or she wouldn't be seeing tomorrow.

The cell was completely secure. The only way she'd get out was if someone released her. Molly knew that her hypnotism hadn't worked the last time she'd tried to use it. Neither had her mind reading. Part of her was tempted to try them again. But the realistic part of her suddenly knew for certain that all her skills had gone. If she wanted to escape, she would have to use her wits.

She went over to the door. 'HELLO!' she shouted gleefully. It took a lot of energy to sound cheerful because she was crying inside. 'HELLO-EEE! ANYONE THERE? THIS ROOM'S SO PRETTY AND SWEET! HELLO! CAN YOU COME HERE A MOMENT, PLEASE?' Molly heard someone stir in the corridor outside. She began singing. 'La la la la – life's such fun! Full of beans, full of sun, HOW I LOVE!' One of the bodyguards appeared at the door's small window. 'Oooh, hello!' Molly smiled happily at the man. 'I have a little problem,' she said sweetly. 'I really, really, really need to go to the, hmmm, what's it's called in Japanese? . . . I know, toilee.' Molly

179

sang the word as though she was the happiest person in the world. The man outside grunted, judging that Molly was definitely still under the influence of the tea that Mr Proila had given her. Molly heard keys rattling, then the sound of metal slotting through metal.

'OK, OK.' The man nodded.

Molly gave him a big hug. Then she made an 'I'm desperate' face and said again, 'Toilee, toilee, toilee!' as cutely as she could.

The guard led her up the stairs towards the room where Molly had got changed. She walked past her own clothes that were folded on a bench. As she did she thought what a fool she had been for not being suspicious of Mr Proila. She stepped past the guard into the bathroom, humming and smiling all the way.

She picked up the toilet roll. 'Um . . . and hmmm.' She coughed, pointing at the loo.

The guard nodded grimly and shut the door. Molly decided not to lock it. Instead she noisily put the lid of the toilet up. Then, seeing some buttons on the control panel beside the loo, she chose the one that had a fountain symbol. Immediately the noise of recorded running water designed to cover up the noise of a person using the loo, sang out.

Molly was shaking from nerves. The guard wouldn't give her long. She only had a few minutes to escape.

There was a lidded wooden bath at the end of the room. Quietly as she could, she stepped on to it and opened the wide window above it. Two metres below was the garden where the apple tree grew. She could jump down, she thought, run across the garden and then try to climb the perimeter wall, but whether she'd manage to escape before the guard realized she'd run away was another question. Molly decided she would take a huge risk. She took the black hair sticks that held up her hair and threw them so that they dropped a few metres away, on the grass below the window. Leaving the window open, Molly got down off the bath and opened it. Then she climbed in and pulled the lid back into place. Then she waited.

For a while everything was quiet, except for the sound of the fake water gurgling from the loo's 'music box'. Molly bit her knuckles. Perhaps she had made a fatal error of judgement. Perhaps things wouldn't go as she'd hoped.

After a short while the guard started to knock at the door. 'Missa Moon?' he asked. Molly lay curled up, trying to make the very bath think that she wasn't there. After a few more calls, she heard the guard open the door, then gasp.

'*Noroi!*' he cursed. Molly then heard his heavy footsteps in the passage and on the stairs. Almost immediately Mr Proila's familiar voice boomed from somewhere in the building.

'*WHAT?!*' There was more thudding of rushing feet and then Mr Proila was in the bathroom too.

'Well, what are you waiting for? Get her! *Kanojyo heru!*'

Molly heard the guard leave the room.

'Stupid fool!' Mr Proila spat. With difficulty he

clambered up on to the lid of the bath. The wood bent and squeaked over Molly's head.

'AAARRGH!' Mr Proila screamed with rage out of the window. Molly trembled. He was so close, and yet totally ignorant of Molly's presence.

And then she felt the pull of the coin. It was just above her head. How she wanted it!

There was a thud as he slumped down to sit on the bath lid. 'We'll get her,' Mr Proila said conspiratorially. Molly realized he was talking to the coin. 'If she escapes, of course the first thing she'll do is find one of her fans. Seek protection. Ha! She won't be protected at all. Far from it. I've got friends in very high places, haven't I? By showing up, she'll be helping me. She'll be arrested and secretly handed back to me. And then? Then – I'll either play music to her till she does exactly what she's told or –' Mr Proila's voice dropped so deep that he sounded like a troll – 'or I'll just dispose of the brat. Chop her up into little bits and scatter her all over Japan for the birds to eat.'

Molly was so scared she thought her heart might stop.

There was silence, and Molly was convinced that Mr Proila had guessed where she was. Then he spoke: 'Message for Miss Sny. Book a show for Friday night. Say that Molly Moon is going to make an appearance. I'll be going onstage with her. I'll be playing too. End of message.' Mr Proila started talking to the coin again. 'With you I'll be able to play every sort of instrument, won't I? It's just you and me now. Those musical instruments should be here any second. Ha! And when they do arrive . . . Wow, wow, wow!'

Mr Proila got off the bath. Molly heard him walking away. 'What will my stage name be?' he mused. 'Tattoo King? Yes.' He went down the stairs. The front door slammed.

Molly was rigid with fear, yet she knew she must get out of the building before Mr Proila came back. She was deeply depressed by the loss of her coin, but also by the loss of all her other hypnotic skills. She had to accept that they were gone. On top of this she was overwhelmed by loneliness. She remembered with shame how she had spoken to Rocky, how she had treated Petula and Gerry. As though the bath had suddenly filled with liquid guilt, she felt herself start to drown in self-loathing. The only saving thought was the idea that the coin had made her behave so badly. But why hadn't she resisted it? Why did she even want it back? Did that show that she was essentially bad? Molly's head swam with feelings of remorse and confusion. But bearing down on her was the knowledge that she had to get out of the tea house before Mr Proila returned.

Chapter Twenty-six

Molly slid the wooden bath lid off, making sure it didn't clatter to the floor.

She couldn't go out of the front door of the building as Mr Proila might still be outside. She climbed back up on the bath, peered out of the window and began to wriggle through it. Holding on to the windowsill, she lowered herself so that the drop was as short as possible. Even so, she thudded hard on to the wet grass. She sprinted across the garden and scrambled over the wall, praying all the while that a guard wouldn't be on the other side to catch her.

Instead, Molly found herself in an ornamental pond filled with white and orange carp. She waded across, the fish scattering about her, and out the other side. Her kimono was soaked and weighed down with water. Gathering the wet material in both hands, Molly ran across another garden, then clambered over a low brambly hedge.

She didn't know where to go. She remembered Mr Proila's words about what he would do if he found her. He'd stop at nothing to make sure that Molly's mouth was gagged to keep the coin's secret.

Trying to calm down, Molly hid for a moment by a bush and tried to work out a plan. She recognized a tall red building in the distance. She knew that the main Tokyo train station was near there. If she could get on a train, at least then she'd be out of Mr Proila's immediate vicinity.

Molly left the garden through a gate and found herself on an empty street. She ran. Was it her imagination or were there people following behind her? She didn't dare look. If she actually saw Proila's guards chasing her, she might freeze. She was sure they were getting closer. Their feet were pounding the pavement. Molly's socked feet slapped the tarmac and her heart raced. The soles of her feet stung. But she didn't care. Nothing mattered except for getting away. Ahead, Molly saw people – ordinary people. Her challenge now was to navigate the crowds without being recognized. She hoped that her dishevelled appearance, her make-up and the speed at which she was careering along would mean no one would realize she was Molly Moon.

Beyond the T-junction she was coming up to was a wide street full of fast-moving cars. A clot of people waited for the lights to change so that they could cross. As Molly approached, the green pedestrian light flashed and the crowd began to surge forward. Molly dived for a gap between two schoolgirls, hurdled over the back wheel of a woman's bike and squeezed past an old lady. She dashed to the other side.

Behind, she was sure she heard cries of complaint as Mr Proila's bodyguards knocked people over.

Molly sprinted down the street towards the red building. She ran across another street, dodging the cars. The noise of screeching brakes and blaring horns filled the air as drivers tried to avoid her.

Molly darted through groups of pedestrians. She curved past women pushing strollers and people wheeling suitcases. Molly saw a sign ahead, in Japanese letters but with an arrow and a picture of a train. In English, it said: 'Tokyo Central Station'.

She hurried towards it, keeping her head down so that people wouldn't recognize her. She paused at a ticket booth and, out of breath, read the information board beside it. 'Tokyo-Kyoto . . . 18:30.' Molly gasped. She pulled some of the yen notes out of her pocket. 'Kyoto, please.'

As she took her ticket and her change and turned away, she saw a sign for the toilets. At the same time she noticed that many people were wearing surgical masks, as Chokichi had told her they do in Japan during the flu season, and she had an idea.

A minute later Molly was coming out of the ladies' toilet with a makeshift mask on. She hurriedly read the electronic information boards, where English and

Japanese were displayed in turn. 'Kyoto, 18.30 . . . 2', the board flashed. Seeing that further down the forecourt was the number two with an arrow beside it, Molly started to run again. The station was full of commuters. They looked at Molly, not because they recognized her but because she was a child alone in wet clothes and no shoes.

There was her train – a smart white bullet train that would take her to Kyoto. Molly ran along platform two, jumped on to the train and quickly slid into a seat. From there she checked the platform and the stairs for Mr Proila's bodyguards.

She saw only one. He was walking past the top of the stairs to the train at the next platform. Molly ducked.

'Please don't guess I'm on this train! Please don't guess I'm on here.'

The doors bleeped and swished shut. A Japanese voice began talking over the train's tannoy. The announcement was then repeated in English. 'This train is about to depart for Kyoto. Journey time: two hours forty minutes.'

The train began to move. Molly willed it to pick up speed. Her nightmare was that it might stop and reverse back to the station.

For a long while Molly stayed rigid. She half expected a hand to come down on her shoulder. But Mr Proila's bodyguard didn't appear.

As she slowly relaxed, Molly shivered. The train was

warm but her clothes were damp and stuck to her. She peeled her socks off. They were black with filth. Her teeth chattering, she gazed out of the window.

The train carved its way between tall futuristic buildings. Gradually, the structures beyond the glass got lower. Finally they hit open countryside and the train switched to top speed.

Molly's bottom lip trembled. She was miserable. She was being hunted and she had no one to turn to for help. She thought of Rocky, of Petula and Gerry, wondering where they were, and then of her parents, and of Forest, Micky and Ojas back home. A painful lump grew in her throat. Teardrops rolled down her smeared white face. She would call home, if only she could remember the number. But right now her head was a storm and the number a blank. What if Mr Proila found out about Molly's parents and got their number, and played music down the phone to them, or played to them over the Internet? They'd be hypnotized by him too and she'd never get home, never feel safe again.

The magnitude of the change that had come over her and of the greed and selfishness that had consumed her when she had the coin, was almost unbelievable. It was only now, with the immediate problems of escaping behind her, that Molly was able truly to reflect upon how the coin had affected her.

Reeling from the shock, Molly pressed her mask up to her face and fell asleep.

*

When she awoke, the train was at Kyoto station. She got up and, with her mask on her face and her head down, she darted towards the door. Once on the platform she bolted for the exit.

She half expected Mr Proila and one of his guards to step across the entrance – a huge, human barrier. He wasn't there, but Molly knew it would be foolish to assume she was safe. She must get out of the station without people seeing her. There were security cameras everywhere. Molly glanced up at one, then wished she hadn't. She could imagine Mr Proila in a police station, watching hidden-camera video footage, saying, 'That's her.'

In her bare feet, Molly hurried away from the station as fast as she could. Scanning the building-lined avenue before her, she saw a small street with food shops and hurried towards it. She ran down it and into an even narrower road. This one was lined with electrical shops, all with TVs and computer monitors in their windows. To Molly's horror she saw herself on these screens. Enthusiastic shopkeepers were playing recorded Molly Moon concerts to lure people into their shops. Like Frankenstein's monster, this twisted version of herself stalked her.

Molly was tempted to go into one of these shops and ask for help. But it was too risky. She ran on, round corners, down an alley and along other back streets. She hoped she wasn't running in circles.

Eventually she came to a dead end. She found her way

blocked by an old wall with ivy growing up it. Beyond were trees. The wall was easy enough to climb. Molly clambered up, swung her legs over the top of the wall and jumped down the other side.

It seemed she was in a graveyard, because there were lots of upright old stones there. A few had Japanese writing on them. They weren't the same shape as gravestones she'd seen before. Some were more like pillars with oval tops, others were like miniature houses. In between were clipped bushes and ornamental trees and well-tended areas of white gravel, and beyond the stones was a very old building.

Molly hid in a tomb shaped like a house, watching the rain as it fell on the grass and the pruned garden. She began to cough. A light went on in the building. She could see a bald-headed person in a brown tunic inside. He looked like a monk or some sort of holy man. Molly wondered how many other monks there were in there. Perhaps she could sneak in through an open window to the food and warmth that she was sure lay beyond. Of course, if she found any clothing as well, that would be even better.

She watched the window like a cat at a mouse hole. Never had the thought of dry clothes and some hot food been so attractive. Night drew in. Molly shivered and coughed and waited.

When the light had gone out and it was completely dark, and wincing at every twig that snapped under her feet, Molly crept towards the building. There was an open window upstairs. Luckily there was a tree close to it and the tree looked easy enough to climb. Molly hitched up her kimono and scaled it. Using a branch as a bridge, she was soon sitting on the windowsill.

The room was dark, and Molly paused. It struck her that this might be the bald man's bedroom. Then her eyes adjusted to the light. She saw that the room was merely some sort of reading room. With her bare feet she was able to slip silently inside. Holding her breath, she stole across the room and peeped around the door. Beyond there was a corridor.

The building was deadly silent. Molly had no idea how many people were in there. But she was desperate for something to eat. She crept down some stairs and along a low-ceilinged passage. All the while she ached to cough, but she managed to keep it in.

She passed an indoor garden. A gnarled tree grew right up through the centre of the building. She could see the starlit sky above. Molly paused for a moment to listen. Then, sure that everyone in the place was asleep, she went on.

On the far side of the indoor garden was a door with a bead curtain. Molly could see a small kitchen.

She crept inside and opened the fridge. There was a bowl of white sticky rice and a dish of tofu. Molly ate it all. She put the bowl and dish back in the fridge, hoping that by the time they were found she would be gone. Then quietly she stole back upstairs and into the reading room. There was a dressing gown on the back of the door.

191

Shaking from cold, Molly took off her wet kimono and put on the dressing gown. Making herself a bed on the floor from a blanket and pillow that she found on the chair, she fell into an exhausted sleep.

Chapter Twenty-seven

When Molly opened her eyes, the bald monk she'd seen the night before sat in one of the armchairs observing her.

'H-have you called the police?' she asked, sitting up.

The old man shook his head. 'Do you think I should?'

'No, please don't.' Molly's voice brimmed with urgency. 'Er, do you like my music?'

The old man scratched his chin. 'Were you playing last night in the garden? I didn't hear music. Heard you arrive though. Saw you hide. Left window open for you and dressing gown and blankets. I am happy you found food.' He started laughing. 'You leave empty bowls in fridge. Very funny!'

Molly shifted uncomfortably on to her elbow.

'You lonely girl. You come to right place. This Buddhist holy place. I am caretaker monk. All alone. You stay here for few days and you find balance. No one find you. You safe.'

Molly coughed. The old man passed her a tissue.

'Blow nose and drink.' He pointed to a steaming cup beside Molly. 'Body recover too. Fix cough. This matcha. Very good Japanese green tea.'

Molly reached for the drink. 'Thank you,' she said. 'And please, please don't ring any police. I am not a lost child.' Molly sneezed. 'The thing is, there is a bad, bad, bad man out there who wants to kill me.' Molly used her finger as an imaginary knife and pretended to cut her neck with it. 'If you report me to the police, he find me and then he kill me.'

'You safe here. Look . . .' The monk pointed out of the window. 'Good day coming. My name Do. See you downstairs.'

Molly watched the man hobble out of the room and she lay back on her pillow. She wondered whether she really was safe.

When she went downstairs, she found breakfast waiting: rice dumplings and some sort of fishy paste. After everything was cleared away, Do stood up.

'Now we do Samu – Zen work ceremony,' he said.

Molly supposed she might as well do whatever the old monk wanted her to do. After all, she had nothing else to do and nowhere else to go. The idea of having nowhere to go frightened her.

Outside, it was a fresh March morning with blue skies. The leaves of the garden were so glossy from the morning sun that it was as if they shone. Over to the side of the monastery was a large expanse of white gravel with a few big stones placed on it.

'Gravel represent sea,' Do said as he led Molly to the garden. 'Rocks round edges like mountains. It like miniature world. See? And spirits live in these rocks, these little mountains. Live in bushes and trees also. This Shinto belief.'

Do went to a narrow upright shed and took out two wooden rakes, each with four prongs.

'We rake gravel. See how beautiful? Look, your steps yesterday mess up gravel. But no problem. I rake every day. Good for soul. You watch, then copy.'

Molly nodded. The old man set to work. He began to go over the whole of the gravelled area, smoothing it out with the back of his rake.

'First clear,' he explained. 'Remove moss with rake and with fingers. This take while. You do too.'

Molly picked up the other rake and began to copy the monk. As the morning sun beamed down on her back, she found herself relaxing.

'So, gravel represent sea and also sea of consciousness,' Do said mysteriously. 'Flatten out like this is good – the movement good for body. The care of the gravel care for soul. This very Zen.'

Molly nodded. 'I've done lots of meditation with a hippy I know,' she said, thinking of Forest, 'but I've never heard about this sort of Zen garden stuff.'

'Ahhhh.' The old monk nodded, smiling sagely. 'So

you meditate! That's why you find me. Your mind clear through meditation. I think you didn't know it, but your mind open. Mind saw this place and led you here.' He raked a bit more, nodding and chuckling to himself. 'Mind more switched on than you think.'

'What would you say if I told you that recently my mind made me do all sorts of things I shouldn't have because it was controlled by a very bad thing? By a bad spirit.'

Do tilted his head. 'I know that many people behave badly because of many things. Hate – and love – can make people behave badly. Love of things like power or money make bad greed. A spirit made you bad, you say?'

'Well –' Molly sighed, feeling suddenly that she could unburden herself – 'there was a thing, a coin with a bad spirit in it that turned me into a monster . . . Can you believe that? I loved the coin for the power it gave me. It made me feel like I was its master, but actually I was its slave. I would have done *anything* to keep it.'

The old man took Molly's chin in his weather-beaten hand and turned her face to look into her eyes. 'So, you have seen dark side of yourself.'

'Yes,' Molly admitted with a gulp. 'And it wasn't nice.'

Do pointed at the ground. 'Gravel all flat. Lines and marks from yesterday gone. Your past is past. Now you have future. You make new lines. Let us make good pattern.'

The old monk stepped towards the corner of the fresh

gravel field and began raking it, making long marks through the white stones.

'Your turn. Rake new lines in The Now.'

Molly copied him. Her lines looked like waves.

After they had finished raking the Zen garden, they both sat on a stone bench and admired the beauty of it.

'It's cool,' Molly said.

The old monk nodded. 'Now, shut your eyes and focus on breath. You clever, so maybe you try this . . . Have in your mind word "AUM". But, and this important, don't say the A, don't say the M, just say the U. U. U. U. OK?'

Molly nodded. She might as well try it. 'U U U U U U U U U U U U U U . . .' Amazingly, she actually liked doing it. She found it relaxing.

'It helps take us to the calm place inside us where we let go of troubles. Good trick to know!' Do said. 'You can even expand AUM to whole of mind so no space for any other thought or feeling. Good, eh?'

'Hmmm.' Molly nodded. 'But, Do, you can't just kind of switch off like that. As soon as you open your eyes, the trouble comes back. I mean, I'm worried. Worried about some boys I know who I was really nasty to. And my dog Petula that I just deserted. There's a bad man out there,' she went on slowly. 'He's got the coin I used to have, and it makes him even more evil than he was before. He wants to control everyone's minds and have everyone in his power.'

'It seems to me,' Do considered, 'that he should not have coin.'

Molly couldn't help smiling at Do's simple answer. She nodded. 'Yes. You're right. I have to get it off him.'

Chapter Twenty-eight

Do's advice to Molly was clear – if she sat quietly and meditated, she would work out how to get the coin back.

Molly hoped Do was right. She knew that the monster that was Mr Proila was growing more and more powerful every day.

On her third day with the monk, Molly sat in the sunshine in the courtyard. Her eyes were shut and she was meditating when she heard a noise in the garden. Opening her eyes, she saw a movement in the juniper bushes. Molly felt the animal fear that she hadn't felt for days – the fear of being chased.

Molly sat frozen, but then she saw two eyes staring straight into hers. She scrambled to her feet.

'Don't be scared.'

A balding, grey-haired man in a tweed suit and black

spectacles stepped out of the bushes. He had a big nose and a very wrinkly face and he was distinctly old-fashioned-looking. His accent was English. The spooky thing was that Molly recognized him – but she could not, for the life of her, think why or how.

She stepped back a few paces.

'Molly, please wait,' the man entreated.

Molly wondered if he was a crazed fan. 'I don't play music any more,' she said. 'I can't help, sorry.'

'No, the coin isn't in your possession any more,' the old man said. 'If it were, I wouldn't be able to be here.'

Molly was immediately suspicious. 'How do you know about the coin?'

The man pulled a large handkerchief out of his top pocket. Wiping his brow with it, he sat down on a low tombstone. 'I know about the coin better than anyone. I'm very sorry . . . I had it made, you see.'

Molly stood stock still. 'Who are you?'

'This is going to sound very strange,' the man said, 'but I'm going to say it anyway. I am your great-great-grandfather, Molly. You might recognize my name. You've seen it in print. I am Dr Logan.'

All at once Molly knew where she had seen this man before. His potato-shaped nose, his closely-set eyes that were very much like her own. She'd seen his face in a black-and-white photograph in the hypnotism book that had taught her her skills: '*Hypnotism: An Ancient Art Explained*. Except this Dr Logan was much older. He looked about seventy, whereas the picture in the book had been of a much younger man.

'You wrote it!' Molly gasped. 'I can't believe it. So . . . so . . . you're time travelling . . .'

'Correct. I'm an old man now. I wrote that book in 1908, when I was fifty. Twenty years ago in my time and life. But of course my time was more than eighty years ago from where we are now. I have travelled from the year 1928, hence my old-fashioned clothes. I've been trying to land in your time for a while, Molly, but, well, I'm getting on a bit and I'm not such a dab hand at time travel as I was, and for a while now you've had the coin, which made it even more difficult. There were times when I tried to get to you, but the coin's repelling barrier wouldn't let me. You might have seen me. In Quito, near that old tramp. Do you remember? And I tried to appear to you on a few occasions on the balcony of that apartment in Tokyo too.'

Molly noticed the old man's hand shake as he took his spectacles off and polished them. He looked worn out.

'I . . . I do remember,' she said, finding it hard to take in everything he was saying. 'I thought you were a fan, a stalker.'

'I kept trying, even though it was impossible. You see, Molly,' Dr Logan explained, 'I had to get to you to try to put right what I made wrong. The coin – I should never have had it made. I got carried away. I thought its existence would be useful. I mistakenly thought that to be able to mesmerize people with just one stroke of a hand over guitar strings, or harp strings, or over the keys of a piano would be a good thing. I thought that evil people could be brought to heel with it – hypnotized into being good. But I never considered the terrible consequences that might come about should a bad person get hold of the coin. And . . . and, anyway, the coin wasn't a great success. It didn't turn out the way it was supposed to. It led people to badness. It made the owner of it selfish and cruel – that wasn't supposed to happen. I wanted to have it so much that I overlooked the danger. Do you know what a numinist is?' Molly shook her head. 'Well, a numinist studies and makes coins. In numinist alchemy, things can go wrong. With that coin, things did go wrong.' He blew his nose. 'I dropped into the time when you had it, Molly, and saw what the coin was doing for you and with you. But I couldn't interfere directly. It made sure I couldn't interfere. Just as it makes sure no one but its current owner can touch it by giving them a painful shock. But now you don't have it and so I can come close and speak to you. That's how I knew you no longer had it in your possession.'

Molly stepped forward and took Dr Logan's hand. 'I know who has the coin. I've been trying to work out how to get it off him, not because I want it for myself – I never, ever want it for myself again. I'm really glad you're here, because I'm sure together we can work out what to do. You look terrible though. You have to eat before anything else. Come on inside.'

'You're right,' Dr Logan admitted. 'I'm famished.' Gratefully he followed his great-great-granddaughter inside.

Chapter Twenty-nine

In the kitchen Dr Logan stood admiring the coffee machine and the cooker.

'I've been to your time before and to other times in the future on many occasions,' he said, 'but this sort of technology never ceases to amaze me. In my day if we're lucky we have a wooden cupboard with big lumps of ice kept in a top compartment to keep everything cool.'

'How far into the future have you travelled?' Molly asked, reaching for some sushi that she and Do had made that morning.

'Well, when I was younger I travelled a fair deal. To the year 10,000. That's thousands of years from today! Imagine!'

'Wow! What was the world like?' Molly asked.

'I only dropped in for a day. Frankly, being too far in the future always scared me. But I was pleased to see that humans hadn't destroyed the world yet.'

'I once went to the year 2,500,' said Molly. 'The Earth had heated up a lot by then.' She passed Dr Logan a wooden plate of sushi.

'I know.' Her great-great-grandfather studied a piece before he ate it. 'It's hot in 2,500, then it cools down again. The world's population shrinks too. There is a massive plague sometime around the end of the millennium. Nasty business.' He sat down at the small table and began to eat. 'Delicious. Very interesting food. By the year 10,000 the plague was history, of course. There were fewer people about though. Medicine is absolutely brilliant by then! All the fuel technologies are very advanced. Clean fuel – no pollution. Fantastic! People become very fond of growing things again. It's a marvellous time. Oh, and people live longer!'

Molly considered her wrinkly, bent, old great-great-grandfather. 'Why don't you go there to live?' she asked. Then she realized that perhaps she had sounded a bit blunt. 'I mean, I hope you don't mind my saying so, but you seem very old. They could help you live longer.'

The old man smiled. 'I have considered it, but, Molly my dear, I would have been lonely. I have my friends in my time, in 1928, you see, and I've had a good life. So dying is not something I mind doing.' He peered through his spectacles at Molly. 'Oh, my lovely great-great-granddaughter, I must say what a pleasure it is to meet you. You are the one who inherited the flair, the genius.

I'm . . .' Dr Logan looked sad and worried for a moment. 'I'm sorry that I have caused you to lose your hypnotic skills. I watched you trying to hypnotize Mr Proila. I saw you through my time-travel bubble . . .'

Molly stared up at him. 'Have I?' she said. 'Have I lost them forever? I knew they'd gone, but I thought . . . Is it permanent?'

'They may come back, my dear. You might find that your memory for numbers and names isn't so good for a while too. My powers were diminished by the coin and I did get them back. But I used the coin only for a very short time. I felt how dangerous it was and resisted it. I hid it for a decade and then lost it. I was lucky. The coin sucked so much more from you. The more you took from it, the more it took from you.' He paused. 'I expect you made brilliant music.'

Molly perked up. 'It was amazing,' she said. 'So good that I even want to hear some of it again now! But I know I mustn't. It's not real.' She hesitated. 'Can I ask you something?'

'Of course, my dear.'

'If you knew the coin was bad, why didn't you materialize in my time *before* I got it and stop me ever having it? Or stop Miss Hunroe having it – or whoever had it before her?'

Dr Logan nodded gravely. 'A combination of reasons. First of all, it is impossible for a time traveller actually to take the coin, or even get close to it. As you now know, I tried to warn you, but to no avail. And I tried to intercept it before Miss Hunroe had it, but it kept swerving me off course. Once she was in the grip of its power I could do nothing. On top of this, because I am old, my time-travel skills are weak. I began to realize that I only had so much oomph. When I saw that you had left the apartment in Japan, it struck me that the most important thing was to find you. And I found you here. The problem is that, being seventy, I do not have endless energy to chase the coin.'

'The coin sent you swerving off course?'

'Yes. It's like an evil hurricane.'

'It was really nice of you to come all this way to help me.' Molly stroked her grandfather's arm. 'But I don't understand why you came here. I haven't got it any more.'

'I know. But you know where it is. I am hoping that you and I now, in the same time as the coin's present time, will be able to work out a way to dupe it. Because if there's one last thing I do in my life, it will be destroying that blasted coin.'

At this point Do came in. Molly introduced him to Dr Logan. Do didn't even flinch when she explained that this old man had come from the 1920s. Instead, he chuckled.

Soon they were all sitting on rock stools around a stone table outside, Dr Logan with a bowl of soup. Molly pointed to the red and green conker-sized crystals that hung on a chain around her grandfather's neck. 'These are the time-travel crystals that I told you about, Do. The cracks in them are actually shut eyes. If a time traveller sends good feelings, proper good feelings, to them, they will open. And when they do the time traveller can go really, really fast through time.'

Dr Logan patted Molly's shoulder fondly. 'I must say again, it is a pleasure to meet you, my dear.'

Molly smiled. 'And me you. I've often wanted to. So, tell me, how did you make the coin?'

'That is a good question,' he replied, his eyes glazing over as he dug into his memories. 'It was a long time ago, when I was much younger. I was fifty-fi– no, fifty-seven. Yes. It was after I wrote the second book.' He chuckled. 'You'll never believe what I did. I followed our ancestors back. Yours and mine, Molly. I went further and further back through time. I saw *my* great-great-grandfather. And I went back further still. Back past the Romans invading Britain! I saw great hypnotists, truly great women and men that were our ancestors. A few were burned at the stake, I have to tell you. People thought them witches or wizards, which of course they weren't. I followed the ancestors who carried the hypnotic gene.'

'Wow!' Molly gasped. 'That must have taken ages!'

'It did. Sometimes the talent seemed to skip a generation and other times it didn't come up so strong. A bit like this nose of ours.' He pointed to Molly's and then to his own potato-shaped nose. 'Not everyone in our family has this nose – nor does everyone have the hypnotic power.

Anyway, on my journeys I came across a woman of the most superb power. She was the finest hypnotist I have ever met. Her powers were extraordinary. They didn't stop at hypnotism – oh no – she was a brilliant time stopper and time traveller, a genius mind reader, a gifted morpher. She could do other things too. A tremendous woman. And it was from her that I got the coin.'

'Where did she get it?' Do asked.

'She made it. Honestly, she was beyond marvellous. She was—'

'Well,' Molly interrupted, 'she's the person we should visit.' Dr Logan spluttered into his soup. Molly looked at him earnestly. 'Can you manage it?'

Her grandfather coughed and dabbed at his mouth with his handkerchief. 'I suppose it would be a good idea to visit her. If . . . if I can locate her.'

'Can you try?' said Molly. 'We could go now. If you've finished your soup.'

Dr Logan's eyebrows arched. 'Now? Hmmm.' He reached for the green crystal around his neck.

'It's the green one we'll be needing to travel back in time,' Molly explained to Do.

Dr Logan nodded, then smiled. He stood up. 'No time like the present. Are you ready?'

Molly stood up too and took his hand.

Her grandfather gazed into the green crystal. All of a sudden the crack on it blinked open and an eye stared out. Dr Logan spoke slowly and determinedly. 'One, two, three . . .'

There was a BOOM as the place where Molly and her grandfather had been was suddenly filled with air.

Dr Logan and Molly were on their way.

Do nodded and shut his eyes.

Chapter Thirty

Rocky, Gerry and Toka sat around a wooden table. Petula was curled up on the matted floor beside them, asleep. In the next room, student sumo wrestlers were practising. The noise of slapping, tussling and thudding penetrated the walls.

The boys had a pile of Japanese newspapers. Toka was reading a section where a photograph of Molly's face smiled out at them.

'It says,' Toka explained, 'the same stuff as the other ones. She was last seen running through the streets of Tokyo, wet and in green kimono, with face painted like geisha. It says police are looking into sightings of this Molly. There are reports that she took the bullet train to Kyoto.'

'Does this one say the same thing about Proila as the others do?' Rocky asked, pointing at a photograph of

Mr Proila on a stage playing a guitar.

'Yes, it's about the fabulous concert he gave, playing guitar, piano and mouth organ.' Toka shook his head. 'Even though he's deaf! Wow! That coin is so powerful!'

'So we're sure then,' Rock concluded. 'Proila now has the coin.' He stroked Petula. 'And Molly, without it, is what?'

'Well, she knows 'is secret, don't she?' said Gerry. ''E'll do anythin' to shut 'er up. No wonder she's runnin'. Poor, poor Molly. I feel so sorry for 'er.'

Toka turned the newspaper to study its front page. 'Bad news about the whales. Still can't believe that.'

'Are you sure you read it right?' Gerry asked.

Toka nodded and reread the headline. 'From today, whale hunting is OK. It new sport and it OK to buy whale meat.'

'Proila definitely had something to do with that,' Gerry observed. 'All he needed to do was play music to the prime minister.'

'What other nasty documents did he get signed?' Rocky wondered. 'Yesterday dogfighting and cockfights were made legal. Today whale hunting. What's tomorrow? We've got to find Molly.'

'Before Proila does.'

'Poor Molly,' said Gerry. 'Where is she ?'

Molly's great-great-grandfather held an invisible lasso firmly around her, as he whizzed her backwards through time. Warm time winds swirled about them as Dr Logan's special crystal took them both back through the centuries. The sky above flickered from light to dark as the transporting bubble that they were in reversed through thousands of days and nights. The countryside around them flashed from dark brown to golden to green as the seasons changed in reverse and the plants died and grew and then sprouted.

Molly looked at her grandfather's kindly face as he concentrated. She watched as he judged the right moment to stop.

'This should do it,' he said, his eyebrows lifting. He smiled at Molly and brought them to a 'time hover', which meant that they were hovering in the time but not yet visible. They looked about them.

'Coast seems clear,' Dr Logan said. 'Ready?'

With a BLIP their bubble popped. They were standing in the countryside in tall grass. It was summer and the meadows were in full bloom. Above was a cornflower blue sky. Instead of the buildings of Kyoto, and Do's monastery, tree-filled countryside ran to distant hills.

'We have arrived,' Dr Logan declared. 'This is the time of the marvellous woman I told you about. It's the eleventh century. She doesn't live in Japan though.'

'Oh? Where does she live?'

'Towards Europe, over where Sardinia is going to be.'

Molly frowned, worried. 'Shouldn't we go to the far future to get a super-fast plane to Sardinia?' she suggested. It occurred to her that maybe Dr Logan, old and tired as he was, had miscalculated. He might not have enough energy to go to the future now and then to Sardinia and then to return Molly back to her own time again. 'I mean, in the eleventh century in Japan,' she said, 'probably the only way to get about is by horse or donkey or ox cart.'

'Yes, or by boat . . .' Dr Logan seemed distracted. With his right hand he was digging about in his jacket pocket. 'Don't worry, Molly, we shan't use any of those methods.' He found what he was looking for – a white oval stone that he held up for Molly to see. The disc was about as long as his index finger. It was as slim as a slice of cucumber, slightly thicker towards its centre. It reminded Molly of the dried cuttlefish she'd seen in birdcages for parrots or budgerigars to peck at, except it was smooth. Dr Logan attached the stone to a chain around his neck. 'It's a "floom" – well, that's what I call it.'

'What does it do?'

'It will get us to Fritha. She's the coin-maker ancestor I told you about. Now, Molly, please be quiet a moment, as I really have to concentrate to do this. It's frightfully difficult.' He eyed Molly. 'You are familiar with meditation, aren't you?'

'Yes.'

'Good, thought you would be. Meditation is the way. First we will get ourselves into what I call the Space Water. We will find the right super-highwave to ride. Once we're on that, it should only be a few moments before we are on the island that will one day be Sardinia.'

For the second time Molly doubted the old man. She had no idea what he was talking about. 'What is a super-highwave?' she asked, scepticism audible in her voice. 'And how do we ride one? It sounds like we're about to go surfing.'

'Yes, surfing, that strange sport invented by the Polynesian people way back in the distant past. That is similar to what we are going to be doing now.'

Molly's eyes widened. 'Really?'

'So,' her grandfather went on, 'we have no time to waste, especially as I'm on a roll, as I think you say. You must shut your eyes. Focus on a word that will take you into a nice quiet place inside yourself.'

'Into a trance?' Molly asked.

'Yes, sort of. I suppose you've done that all your life.' Dr Logan closed his eyes.

Molly nodded. She shut hers.

'Good,' her grandfather began. 'So, we'll go deeper if we can, deep into the quietest places of our minds. Relax.'

Molly did as she was told. She thought of the AUM word Do had taught her and said it over and over again in her mind. As the sound filled her, she felt herself being propelled deeper into herself. At first she heard the chirping of birds as they flitted about and the sounds of the wind in the grass, but she soon stopped hearing anything. Her grandfather's voice came loud and clear to her as though he was speaking from right inside her mind.

'Imagine the floom I showed you, Molly. Imagine it as large as a surfboard. Imagine it laid out before you now. Do you see it?'

'Yes.'

'Good. Now step on to it.'

Molly tried but couldn't see herself actually on the stone board. Her grandfather put his hand under her elbow. 'You need a little help. By making contact, you get help from me. Now you are on the board.' In her mind, Molly saw that she was. 'You do not need to look at me,' her grandfather added. 'I am on it too. Are you ready?'

Molly kept her mind focused on the task ahead. She concentrated on the white milkiness of the imagined surfboard under her feet. And then the darkness around the board began rushing, and the board began to tilt and move, as though the darkness all about was some sort of wave tunnel and they were riding through it.

Molly was nervous of falling off yet she knew this was unlikely, as under her elbow she could feel the firm grip of her grandfather's hand. The swirling wave tunnel swished about them faster and faster. The stone surfboard cut through it sharp and silent.

'Whoa!' her grandfather shouted.

Molly kept her focus on the board but at the same time turned to 'look' at her grandfather, without opening her eyes. There he was behind her, in his tweed suit, staring out in front of him with an expression of glee on his face.

'Nearly there!' he exclaimed.

'How do you know?'

'I gave the board instructions, and now I can sense we are near,' he replied. 'Ah!' He took his hand away from Molly's elbow. 'Now, keep your eyes shut and listen; feel the air.'

Molly did as she'd been told. Gone were the sounds of birds and rustling grass. Instead there was the chirping of crickets. Molly could feel hot sun beating down on her head and shoulders.

'Open your eyes!'

Chapter Thirty-one

Molly was amazed. The landscape had meta-morphosed. Now there was craggy granite all about, rocks that had been moulded by the elements so that they resembled animals and faces. Molly and Dr Logan were standing on a hillside with dramatic views down towards an expanse of silvery-blue sea. The ocean disappeared into the horizon.

'Is this Sardinia? The place you made the coin?' Molly said in awe.

'Yes. Come with me.'

Molly stood up and wiped her eyes. 'But I can't believe it. We've sort of teleported here. It's incredible.'

'Teleporting is one way of putting it,' the old man agreed. 'I like to call it "space surfing" or "flooming", but you can make up your own name for it if you like.' He pointed to the hilltop. 'I hope she's in.'

Molly followed Dr Logan up a dry, stony track. The path wove its way between hardy hedges and bushes and mountain flowers. Insects buzzed and grasshoppers leaped through the grass.

Then, for no reason at all, Molly felt her hair stand up on end and her stomach dip.

'Try to ignore it,' Dr Logan said. 'It's not pleasant, I know; trust me, in a minute it gets worse. Just think of straight lines and you'll be fine.'

'What is it?' Molly said, clutching her stomach. It felt as though it was doing somersaults.

'It's the "*scutem*". *Scutem* is a Latin word. It means shield. She instils rocks with a sort of repelling power; then they become *scutem*. They put people off the place. I think those might have something to do with it.' He pointed to a rock that looked like an oddly shaped horse and another that could have been a fossilized gorilla. Molly frowned and concentrated on lines. Sure enough it helped. As soon as they'd passed the weird rocks, the horrible feeling stopped.

Dr Logan and Molly walked on through a stand of cypress trees. They came out on to a small, cliff-like ledge. It looked over a valley that brimmed with green-leafed trees. To the left was a large cave. Above it, the crags had eroded to look like an eagle's head.

'There! That is where she lives.'

'Our . . . our . . . great-super-great-grandmother?' Molly asked.

'Yes – Fritha.'

The path towards the cave was gravelly and well trodden, with clumps of sweet-smelling herbs growing beside it.

'She's a herbalist too,' Dr Logan said.

They reached the cave entrance, where a bell hung. Dr Logan pulled its string so that it swung and rang out.

'Hello!' his voice echoed. No one answered. 'Oh dear,' Dr Logan said. 'I do hope she hasn't gone on a trip!'

'We could always zip forward a month or so if she has,' Molly pointed out.

Then she turned and looked along the cliff path. An elderly woman in a green cloak and a long hessian skirt was walking towards them. She carried a wicker basket overflowing with plant cuttings. Pausing, she put her hand to her forehead to shield her eyes from the sun, and peered at Molly and her grandfather.

Her face was like a turtle's, thick-skinned and brown, and her eyes were green and sparkled in the Sardinian sun. Close up she smelt of bonfires. When she spoke, she had an Irish accent.

'Dr Logan? Is that you?' she said.

'Yes.'

'You've taken a long time to return. You were a young man yesterday.'

'I know. All the time travelling has aged me.' Dr Logan turned to Molly. 'You see, I was here yesterday. But then I went back to my time, and many years have passed. Molly, meet Fritha; Fritha, meet Molly Moon. Molly is a descendant of ours and, I have to tell you, of all the people I have traced that carry the hypnotism gene she is the most talented . . . since you, of course.'

Molly shook her head. 'Maybe I was,' she corrected Dr Logan. 'But you forget – I've lost all my hypnotic skills since . . .'

'Ah yes, yes,' Dr Logan remembered.

The old woman smiled, her tanned face creasing. She put down her basket and placed her hands on Molly's shoulders. 'Pleased to meet you, girlie,' she said. She nodded at Dr Logan. 'Looks like you, too! Extraordinary!' Then she narrowed her eyes and spoke to Molly's grandfather. 'So, what happened with the coin? Did it sort out lots of problems for ya? Judgin' from your ambitious talk yesterday, I expect yous have a wonderful, harmonious society now that all badness has been hypnotized away.'

Dr Logan looked down at the ground. 'It didn't go quite to plan, I'm afraid,' he admitted.

Fritha frowned. 'Ah, then we'd better go inside for a nice cup o' nettle tea.'

They followed Fritha into the first part of her cave. Here, some smouldering embers nestled in a dip in the cave wall. Fritha took a stick, one that was wider at one end like a baseball bat. She dipped this in the glowing embers and it lit. She then led them to a passage beyond, bearing her flaming torch to show them the way.

'Pine sap,' she said. 'It burns very well and doesn't go out. A man who comes to me for my headache cure pays me in torches that he has coated with the sap. They don't last forever, nothin' like your futuristic light bulbs, Molly, but he brings me lots.' She rummaged in her pocket and handed Molly a strip of woody stuff. 'He brings me pine root to chew too. Full of vitamins. Try it.' Molly put it in her mouth. It was sweet in an earthy way. 'Don't swallow it though,' Fritha said. Then she added, 'That outfit you have on, Molly. It looks Japanese.'

'Yes.' Molly had forgotten that she was still in a kimono. 'It's very comfy actually.'

The passage went on, around a corner and then deeper into the hillside. In one place there was a side cave. Molly caught a glimpse of chairs and a table there. Fritha took them towards a patch of light at the end of the tunnel. It grew bigger and bigger as they approached it. Finally the space opened up. They found themselves in a church-sized cavity, where stalactites hung from above and light poured in from a crack near the top of the rocky ceiling. At the far end, more light came into the cave from an opening to the outside surrounded by tall rocks where vines hung down. Water, a natural spring, Molly supposed, came from a crack in this rock, collecting in a small pool beneath it, where it also drained away.

The place smelt mossy, but also of herbs. This was because in the centre of the cave there were heavy wooden tables covered in plants – live and dried – and stones covered in moss. Mixed in with these things were white skulls of animals and glass vessels full of coloured liquids. To the side of the cave was a fireplace set in a dried clay surround. A long narrow chimney carried smoke out through the roof.

Fritha set down her basket and put a cast-iron pot of water on to boil. 'Hungry?' she asked. 'I've made some soda bread.'

'No. No, thank you,' Dr Logan replied. Molly shook her head.

She observed her grandfather's face. She could see that he was embarrassed by what he knew he had to ask Fritha. And, though actually he looked the same age as Fritha, he was acting a bit like a naughty boy who'd come to an adult to own up.

Fritha could obviously sense all of this too for she began to chuckle.

'Oh, Doctor! Maybe it's better Molly explains what ya've come for. I have a feelin' it's about the coin.'

'Are you reading my mind?' Dr Logan asked nervously.

'Oh no! Let me make your tea, then Molly can tell me.'

Molly noticed Fritha's distinct Irish accent again. 'Are you . . . are you Irish?' she asked.

'Yes, wee girl, sure I am.'

Molly thought. 'Did you come here by . . . boat? I mean, Sardinia's a long way from Ireland.'

'How did you get here?' the old woman asked.

'We . . . we . . . er . . . did the space-surfing tunnel thing,' Molly replied.

'Exactly how I got here meself. My grandfather used to bring me here when I was a child. Then back home to Ireland for the summer there. Ya see, this cave is special – an' the weather's a hundred times better than back home, wouldn't you agree?'

'Very sensible,' Molly said admiringly. 'Where did you get your floom from?'

The old woman put her hands on her hips and considered Molly. 'Aha. So that's what you've come for?'

She pulled the scarf from around her neck to reveal a collection of stones and crystals and a couple of coins that hung there on a chain. Among them was a white disc just like Dr Logan's. 'I may be old, but I'm afraid I can't give you mine, Molly. I may need it still.'

'Oh no! I don't want that,' Molly assured her. 'I was just wondering about the flooms. I mean, where do they come from?'

'They find their way to their owners. Just as the time-travel crystals do. All charms seem to work like that. That's all I know. I found mine here in this cave.' She poured some hot water into the teapot. 'One day, if you ever get one, maybe you can travel back in time and trace it back to its origin. Then you'd know where it came from for sure.'

'I don't think I'll be doing that. I've lost my powers,' Molly said.

The old woman's eyebrow arched. 'Oh yes,' she said, glancing at Molly. 'You said. And how did that happen?'

Chapter Thirty-two

Molly told Fritha about her time with the coin.

Fritha was silent for a moment as she stirred the nettles in the teapot. Then, 'Oh dear,' she said. 'I had a feelin' it was goin' to be trouble.' She poured the tea into china cups. 'Do you like these?' she said, distracted. 'I got them from a palace in the seventeenth century. They're French. Where was I? Oh yes, the coin. I feared as much after you left, Doctor. Had nightmares about the coin last night in fact. We had great intentions, but were too ambitious. I wonder where I went wrong? I'm wondering whether I shouldn't have eaten those wood mushrooms yesterday. I was sure they were safe but they made me feel a bit odd. Maybe that's why the coin was bad. But I can't make it vanish, if that's what you were hopin'. The best thing is for you to get it off whoever has it now, take it far into the future and dispose of it there. Drop it in the sea, somewhere deep, or take it into space. You can't melt it down. It won't melt, you know.'

Dr Logan sighed and took his teacup. 'Getting it is the problem. Might you be able to change the coin's . . . erm . . . "rules", as it were?'

The old woman shook her head. She beckoned for Molly and Dr Logan to follow her outside. 'Can't reverse the rules,' she said, sitting down on an old tree stump.

Molly and Dr Logan sat down. For a moment everyone looked about them, watching small birds flit around the top of the ivy-covered light well, where they had built their nests.

'I'm a fool,' Fritha said. 'I'm so sorry. What a mess. I should never have made it. I can't think how to help.'

Dr Logan sipped at his tea. 'There must be something we can do. The problem is getting the coin back.'

Molly sat with her cup and saucer on her lap, watching the birds, two brown birds in particular. All of a sudden, their similarity to each other gave her an idea. 'I know what we can do,' she said. 'Make another coin.'

'Another coin?' Dr Logan and Fritha said in unison.

'Yes, another one. One that has the same pull as the first – that looks almost the same – but that is different.'

'Oh my word!' Dr Logan exclaimed. 'I'm not sure we should make any more coins, after the last one.'

'Och, they're not always bad, Doctor,' Fritha said indignantly. 'Honest. Go on, Molly.'

Molly elaborated. 'Well, the one thing Mr Proila might give up his coin for is another coin that is just as powerful.

Make a coin that has the same sort of magnetism, or greater magnetism than Mr Proila's. But this other coin would need to *do* something to him so that he gives us the music coin, or loses it.'

'That's a bit too precise an instruction to put in a coin,' Fritha said.

Molly shrugged. Everyone was quiet, thinking hard. Molly glanced up at the birds again. It was then that she noticed a small blue bird sitting there doing nothing. She almost spilt her tea as a brilliant idea hit her. 'I know what would work perfectly,' she said excitedly. 'The other coin should just make Mr Proila want to do *nothing*.'

'Nothing?' Dr Logan echoed. 'What about eating, drinking, sleeping?'

'Well, could you make it so that he had those, um . . .'

'. . . impulses.' Dr Logan supplied the right word.

'Yes, those impulses. We don't want to kill him. It is very important that you make it so that me and Dr Logan can be near it. I mean, we won't touch it, but we need to carry it in a pouch or something. Can you make it like that, Fritha?'

Fritha began to undo one of the plaits in her grey hair and then retwist it as she thought. 'Hmm. I like your cogitations, Molly. I reckon it could work. I rebuilt the smeltin' furnace last night.' She pointed to the edge of the rocky light-well, where there was a strange-looking mound with bellows attached to it. 'And I've got everythin' I need to get to work. But –' she shook her head – 'there is a risk. There is a chance that this coin won't be perfect either. I mean, with a tall order like this, things can go wrong.' She clapped her hands. 'But it is worth a try. Look, Doctor, I still have the wax left from yesterday.'

She brought a parcel of damp material over and unwrapped its contents. 'This is modellin' wax, Molly. I will make a coin that looks similar to the other coin – make it in wax. What image should I model on to it? Yesterday's coin had a musical note. What do you think represents nothin'ness?'

'A circle?' Molly said. 'Or . . . nothing ?'

'I'd prefer an image. It's better for carrying the power. So a circle it is. Dr Logan, if you take Molly out of the other side of the cave to get firewood, I'll model the coin.'

Molly was amazed by how swiftly Fritha seemed to have decided that the idea was a good one. 'Do you think it'll work?' she asked.

'Can a parrot be taught to ride a bicycle?' Fritha replied.

Dr Logan and Molly left the old woman. Taking two wicker baskets they retraced their steps and set off for the woods.

Molly breathed in the pine smell and thought how lovely this place was and how intriguing Fritha was and she wished they could stay with her for days. Then she and her grandfather collected firewood. Molly noticed how old and stiff his body was and she made an extra effort so that he wouldn't tire himself out.

It took them half an hour to fill the firewood baskets. By the time they had lugged them back to the cave, Fritha had finished making the wax coin. It lay on a table, on a clean piece of linen. It had sticks of wax stuck to its bottom edge so that on its side it looked like a coin with six roots, and another widening stack of wax stuck out from its top. Fritha was leaning over a wooden bucket, stirring a thick sloppy mixture with a stick.

'What's that?' Molly asked.

'Oh . . .' Fritha glanced up, her face red from all the exertion. 'It's a sort of clay soup. I'll pat it about the coin while it stands on those wax legs. It'll start dryin' straight away. Then I'll put it in my bakin' oven for a couple of hours. The clay will harden, and the wax will melt and dribble out. And then inside will be a cavity – a hole, shaped exactly like our coin. Clever, eh?'

'Then what do you do?'

'Then we will smelt the gold –' Fritha pointed to the mound at the edge of the light-well, 'but we'll have to use the other oven, the really, really hot furnace over there for that.'

Molly shuddered. 'It would be nasty if you got burned.'

'It's not the handlin' of the molten gold that's dangerous, Molly. I'm good at that. No, the dangerous part is imbuing the coin with the power that we want it to have. I obviously got it wrong last time. This time it needs to be perfect. No more evil coins.' She shook her head.

She looked at the firewood that Molly and Dr Logan had collected. 'Right, let's start the big furnace. We'll have to keep feedin' her – a mixture of firewood and charcoal.'

Soon the furnace was going. Fritha showed Molly a

small cast-iron dish with a lip for pouring on one side, like a little jug.

'This is the crucible. Cast iron takes a higher heat to melt than gold so that's why we melt the gold in it.'

'How long will the furnace take to get hot enough?' Molly asked.

'Och, not long now. Now, let's go and find our gold.'

Fritha bellowed the furnace fire a few more times and then she went inside. Molly followed her. They passed Dr Logan, who was now dozing in a large comfortable armchair just inside the cave.

'Let him rest. He came with me to get the gold yesterday, so he doesn't need to see it.'

'See what?'

'The mineral cave.'

Chapter Thirty-three

Molly walked behind Fritha past the central herb table and past the fireplace to the entrance of an inner cave where Fritha lit a torch.

Steps had been hacked out of the sloped floor. They paved the way into a tunnel that went deep under the ground. The walls were damp and clammy, but the air was cool. Molly followed the old woman down, wondering what would happen if her torch went out.

Fritha turned to look at her and began laughing. 'Don't you worry, I'd feel me way back. I know this place like the back of me hand!'

'Have you read my mind often since I got here?' Molly asked.

'No, just the once, when I first saw you outside the cave. I wanted to check who you were. Though it was obvious you weren't from this time because of your clothes. You were thinkin' about how much I look like a turtle!' Fritha patted Molly reassuringly. 'Don't worry! I do!'

'So you're a hypnotist, a time stopper, a time traveller and a mind reader,' Molly said, smiling, as they walked. 'Can you morph?'

'Of course!' Fritha laughed. 'I'm a floomer too. And a coin caster, a weather turner, a stoner.'

'A stoner?' Molly was puzzled.

'It's like it sounds. I can turn meself into a stone. Don't like doin' it much. It's a bit frightenin'. Turnin' into stones always makes me feel like I'm a gravestone! An' turnin' into a chair or a table isn't much better. It's like morphing, but you turn into an inanimate object.'

'Was it in Dr Logan's book?'

'Oh, I don't know, dearie. I didn't learn things from a book. My grandfather taught me.'

'Dr Logan said you are the best hypnotist ever.'

'Oh no. There have been others just as good as me. Me great-uncle, for instance, he was a genius. He found this place. He's your relation too.'

Molly followed her grandmother down the passage. At one point it grew so narrow that they had to squeeze themselves through it. Eventually they reached a large cave.

Fritha lit some more torches. A high dome curved over them. A silvery pool, like a blob of mercury, lay before them. The nearest walls were streaked with gold and on the far wall were paintings of wild animals – bears, lions and horses.

'Those are thousands of years old,' Fritha said. She directed her torch at the water. 'And what do ya see there?'

Molly looked. Under the still surface, things were flashing and glinting. Gems and crystals. Dotted about were lumps of gold and silver!

'Choose a piece of gold. Go on, get a good lump, one that will do as I tell it!'

'What? Just fish it out?'

'Yes.'

Molly stared into the water. 'Are those time-travelling gems and time-stopping crystals?'

'Yes. There are a lot here.'

'Where do they come from?' Molly asked, wondering for a moment whether she was actually awake. 'How do they get here?'

'It's a mystery.'

For a moment Molly stood stock still, absorbing the magical atmosphere of the cave. Then, spotting a nice round lump of gold, she stepped into the cool water. She waited for the ripples to clear, then she bent down and scooped it out.

Fritha took a small stone bucket from the edge of the cave and scooped some water from the pool. 'Good girl. Come on then.' She extinguished the cave's wall torches. As the flames spluttered, the cave pictures flickered, so that the animals on the walls seemed to come alive. Molly took a last look at this amazing place before following Fritha out.

'Don't you ever have problems with people finding the cave?' Molly asked as they retraced their steps.

'This is a remote place. Over the years a few people have found it – but as hypnotists have always been the guardians o' the cave none of them have ever spread the news o' the place. I feel sorry for the ones I've had to deal with. They are so excited to find the gold. I feel mean, havin' to blank their minds and take all their thrill away, but it has to be done.'

Molly held the lump of gold in her hand. It reminded her of the music coin.

'Beware,' Fritha advised. 'The cave gold is powerful stuff. Don't let it make you want it.'

'Right . . . OK.' Molly nodded back. 'Definitely don't want the same trouble as last time.' Fritha laughed. 'You know, Fritha, that last coin sucked all my powers away.'

Fritha stopped laughing. 'I know, and I'm sorry.'

Back in the main cave, Fritha placed her stone bucket down by the furnace and tended to the fire, feeding it more charcoal, while Molly gave the bellows a good working.

Over the next hour she and Molly took it in turns to keep the flames raging. Eventually Fritha was satisfied. Putting large thick cotton mitts on, she went to the other oven, lifted out the clay mould and carried it over to the furnace.

'Here is best. For the gold pouring,' she said, putting the mould on the ground.

Fritha gingerly picked up Molly's chosen lump of gold and placed it in the iron crucible. Then, gripping the edge of it with a pair of pliers, she carefully placed the crucible into the furnace.

'How long will it take?' Molly asked.

'Not long. The furnace is like an inferno – that gold will melt like ice in the sun.'

While they waited, Fritha made more tea and woke Dr Logan with a cup. He sat up and watched with interest as she got on with her task. She took the crucible out of the furnace.

To Molly's surprise, Fritha didn't pour the gold into the mould. Instead she tipped a small amount into the water she'd brought from the gem cave in the bucket. Instantaneously, steam rose and hissed as the drop of gold cooled. Fritha put the crucible back in the furnace. She then put her hand into the stone bucket and scooped out the now-cold gold and popped it into her mouth. She sat on a stool beside the furnace with her eyes shut, sucking the metal as though it was a boiled sweet.

After ten minutes of this, during which Molly and Dr Logan kept completely silent, Fritha opened her eyes. There was no expression in them. She reached for the pliers and once more pulled the crucible out of the furnace.

She took the small lump of gold from her mouth and placed it in the pool of hot liquid gold in the iron crucible. Like butter melting in a hot frying pan, the lump disappeared. Now Fritha poured all the gold into the mould.

'It's full. That will do.' She looked up at the darkening sky. 'You twos should stay the night. The coin will be ready by the mornin'.'

Chapter Thirty-four

'Wild strawberry jam!' Fritha said, dolloping some on to Dr Logan's and Molly's plates at breakfast.

They sat at a table that was laid with china and silverware that Fritha had brought back from her trips to the future.

'Do you like the toast rack?' she asked. 'Got it from a very modern house in Paris in the 1970s.'

Molly nodded. 'They'd call that groovy,' she said.

'Groovy,' Fritha repeated. Molly smiled.

'I'm looking forward to seeing the coin,' Dr Logan said, munching away.

'How will ya carry it?' Fritha asked.

'I'll take it,' Molly offered. 'In something though. I don't think we should touch it.'

'No. Definitely not,' Fritha agreed. 'It's made so that

the person who touches it and holds it for more than a minute owns it. Very soon after that, they won't want to give it up. If you carry it in this –' Fritha went to her table in the cave and rummaged about before coming back with a leather pouch – 'you will be safe.'

After breakfast Fritha fetched the mould and placed it on the table. She took a little metal hammer from her pocket. Her eyes lit up. 'I can feel it through the clay – do you?'

Both Molly and Dr Logan put their hands up to the clay.

'Makes me feel a bit sleepy,' Molly said.

'It's powerful,' yawned Dr Logan.

'Good.' Fritha smiled. 'I will say goodbye to you both now. Because in a minute you twos will have to move swiftly.' She came over to Molly and embraced her. 'Sorry I made a coin that turned ya bad for a while, dearie – that drained ya of your powers. I'm afraid I'm not perfect and neither are me coins.'

Molly shook her head. 'Don't worry,' she said.

Fritha then took Molly's face in her hands. 'If you ever do get your powers back, please come and visit me again. It was lovely meetin' you.' She kissed Molly on each cheek.

She turned to Dr Logan and hugged him fiercely. Taking a bunch of dried herbs from her apron pocket she gave them to him. 'You should take these for your heart. I sense it is weak.' Without waiting for a response she went on, 'And remember, you twos, the moment the coin is finished, we'll put it in the pouch, then you must leave,

before it tires ya. I will have to file off its rough edges.'
She pointed to an antiquated filing wheel. 'Then it will be
done and away you go.'

Dr Logan nodded. He went to stand beside Molly and
took the white disc that hung round his neck between his
fingers.

'I am ready,' he said. 'The floom is ready, Molly.
Once you have the coin in the pouch, take my hand and
put yourself in a trance and we will go. And thank you,
Fritha.' Dr Logan shut his eyes.

Fritha began chipping. The clay broke away from the
coin inside it as easily as dried mud from around a rock.
The coin was slightly uneven around the edges, but Fritha
soon sorted this out by holding it with pliers and applying
her file. Finally, still gripping it with the pliers, she popped
it in the leather pouch and handed it to Molly.

'Goodbye, me dears.'

Molly nodded. She took her great-great-grandfather's
hand, shut her eyes and concentrated as she had done
before. In her mind she saw the surfboard and she stepped
on to it.

'Good,' she heard Dr Logan say. At once they were off.

Chapter Thirty-five

'Y ou can open your eyes,' Dr Logan said.

Molly recognized the landscape. They were back in the field where Do's monastery would eventually be.

Dr Logan reached for his red time-travel crystal. With a BOOM, they were gone.

Now they were travelling forward through the centuries. The landscape about them flickered as the seasons and the years changed. Finally the monastery's stone walls appeared.

'Nearly there!' Dr Logan proclaimed. 'Let's land now. A day or so out won't matter.'

With a POP, Dr Logan let the time-travel bubble go. All at once they were both standing in the sunshine.

Molly dropped the leather pouch with the coin inside it and breathed a huge sigh of relief.

Do wandered out of the monastery garden, hoe in hand.

'Wah!' he cried in shock. 'You give me big fright.' Then he smiled. 'You gone four days. Success?'

Molly rushed up to Do and gave him a hug. 'I met my ancestor,' she said. 'And we've made a new coin. It's in the sack.' She pointed to the pouch. 'It makes the owner want to do nothing. Isn't that cool? It's powerful, Do!'

'Ah! Clever,' Do replied, smiling. 'And I find out things,' he said. 'I read papers. Wait here.'

He went back inside and moments later came back with a pile of Japanese newspapers. He pointed to an article in one that showed Mr Proila's photograph.

'Look. Proila man play concert three nights ago. Big audience. Big hit. But this part very interesting for you.' Underneath there was a photograph of Chokichi and Hiroyuki. Another picture showed Toka in a sumo outfit in front of an old-fashioned building. 'This sumo school in Tokyo. Boys at sumo academy live like monks! Toka, this boy, I think he no listen to Mr Proila music. And I think he friend of your lost friends. Look.' Do pointed at the corner of the picture. 'I think those little furry things dog ears. Maybe that your dog Patili.'

'Petula!' Molly corrected him with a gasp. She peered at the photograph. 'Amazing, Do. I think you're right.' She turned to Dr Logan. 'I don't suppose . . .'

'Of course,' her grandfather said, nodding. 'We will leave immediately. I just need the address of the place, then I can think it to the disc.'

Do read the address out to him.

'Good. Thank you so much, Do.' Dr Logan smiled at the old monk. 'We'll see you later. Thank you.'

Molly gave Do another hug. 'When I see you again, hopefully it will be with good news!'

She picked up the pouch, took her grandfather's hand and shut her eyes too.

The world tunnelled around.

They hadn't travelled far when Dr Logan squeezed Molly's shoulder. 'I'm going to slow us down! Take a look!'

Molly opened her eyes. She saw how the 'walls' of the space wave that they were surfing through were transparent. She could see houses and gardens. It was as if she and her grandfather were moving on a train, but one made entirely of glass.

It was amazing. They sliced through the air and even through buildings, through cars, through people. When Dr Logan brought them to a very slow pace, it was as if they were surfing alongside people who were walking along pavements. Molly found herself right beside a couple of schoolchildren who were swinging satchels.

Then Dr Logan sped up again, slowing down only at the front door of the sumo academy. Judging the coast clear, he let them arrive. The ground felt firm again under their feet.

'Important to know,' Dr Logan said to Molly as they both surveyed the building in front of them, 'that space surfing is dangerous. If you fall at any point, you fall into the exact place you are passing through. So, for instance, you wouldn't want to fall off in the middle of concrete. Or on a busy road, or over a river or a sea.'

'Glad you didn't tell me that before!' Molly winced as she thought of what might have happened.

Chapter Thirty-six

As they walked to the front doors of the sumo academy, Molly felt her stomach tighten with nerves. Although she longed to see her friends again, she was afraid that Petula, Gerry and Rocky (if he had somehow managed to find the others) would hate her now. Molly steeled herself to expect the worst. Even if she explained how the coin had worked, would they ever properly forgive her? Maybe they'd think that deep down she must be bad and that the coin had just brought out that badness. Maybe if one of them had had the coin nothing would have happened. Did she have more badness inside her than they did?

'I'm scared to see them,' Molly confessed to her grandfather.

'It's going to be terrific,' Dr Logan said distractedly, pushing open the door to the school.

Moments later Toka was called from his room.

He looked suspiciously at Dr Logan and then at Molly in her green kimono. And then crossed his arms defensively.

'Yes?'

'Hi, Toka,' Molly began nervously. 'I need to talk to you. I want to put everything right again.'

As though these were some sort of magic words, Toka's hard expression melted. 'Follow me,' he said.

He led Molly and Dr Logan to his room in the back of the building. They stepped inside. Molly placed the bag with the coin in it on the floor, and then she looked up.

Sitting against the far wall, reading comics, were Gerry and Rocky. Petula was asleep beside them.

Molly felt awful. The full impact of her behaviour punched her hard. She saw in this one moment how much she would miss these friends of hers if they dropped her. And the idea of losing them filled her with a dark sadness. Molly didn't want to speak. She wanted to delay them replying to anything she said, for her fear was that they would say, 'Get out, Molly, we don't want you here.'

So what happened next was totally unexpected.

Rocky threw his comic to one side and scrambled to his feet. He rushed towards Molly and wrapped his arms around her.

'We've been so worried about you. I'm so glad you're safe.'

Petula woke up. For a moment she was stunned. Then she saw that her Molly, her real and true Molly, was back. She ran at her. Gerry grabbed Molly around the waist.

Molly hugged them. Before she knew it her face was wet with tears. 'Thank you,' she managed to say. 'You could have hated me. I'm so, so sorry.'

Petula smelt Molly. All traces of the Monster Molly were gone. It was miraculous. As Molly dropped to her knees and hugged Petula and put her face in the black runkles of her furry neck, Petula snuggled her face into Molly's shoulder.

'We couldn't hate you, Molly,' Rocky said. 'Not the real you. It's the coin we hate, not you.'

For a moment there was quiet.

Dr Logan sighed. 'I'm the one who caused the coin to be made, so I'm afraid I'm to blame for it. It was a stupid mistake.' He paused. 'I'm Dr Logan,' he explained. 'Molly's great-great-grandfather, on a time-travel trip from the past. Rocky and Gerry, I presume?' He stepped towards the boys to shake their hands. 'And this must be Petula.'

Petula gave Dr Logan a sniff. Then she noticed that there was a strange new smell in the room. She turned her head and saw that Molly had brought a bag with her and put it on the floor by the door. She could sense something a little like the other coin that had made Molly bad. She went to inspect it. She could smell steamy air curling out of the bag.

'So explain everything,' Rocky said. 'Sit down and tell us, Molly.'

Molly nodded. 'It's a long story.'

For the next hour, as Gerry played with Titch the mouse and Petula sucked on a stone and kept a wary eye on the bag by the door, Molly explained everything. She told them all about Dr Logan and Fritha, and about the old coin and the new one. She apologized for how horrible she'd been to them all. Then Rocky, Gerry and Toka brought Molly and Dr Logan up to speed.

Even though Mr Proila was deaf, his music was evidently remarkably good, for he'd packed the Tokyo Dome twice and the Japanese prime minister was clearly under Mr Proila's power. They told Molly how overnight, cock fighting, whale hunting and the killing and trading of endangered animals had been legalized.

Molly shook her head. 'Well, let's hope that this new coin will be just as strong as Proila's, but in a good way.' Molly went over and picked up the pouch. The children crowded round.

'Let's see it then,' said Rocky. 'Is this one dangerous?'

'Very. No one must touch it,' said Dr Logan. Molly tipped the new coin on to the floor. It rolled into the centre of the group of friends.

'It's got a kind of tug, hasn't it?' Rocky observed. 'It makes you kind of want it.'

'Yes,' Molly agreed. 'But, if you touch it, it'll turn you into a potato.'

Gerry leaned forward to study the coin. Titch darted towards the coin and jumped on it. 'Oh no!' Gerry cried, reaching out. 'Titch!'

Rocky caught Gerry's hand. 'Don't touch him or it.'

'But I don't want Titch to turn into a potato!'

'He won't,' Molly said. She glanced worriedly at Dr Logan. 'But we should get him off it.'

Titch sat on the coin cleaning his whiskers.

Dr Logan frowned. 'Let's watch a moment.'

Then something else happened. Petula, who had been watching and smelling the new coin, and realizing that it was very different to the coin Molly had had before, got up. She dropped the stone she'd been sucking. She looked at Molly and then at the coin and gave a bark. And then she bounded over to the coin, nudged Titch off it and, before anyone could stop her, picked it up in her mouth. She sat down and scratched her ear.

This coin, Petula thought, doesn't have the repelling quality that the last one had had. It tasted sweet, but that was all she got from it. She sucked it for a good few minutes, then whined at Molly.

She shrugged her shoulders and carefully placed the coin on the pouch.

'I don't know what Petula's trying to say to us,' Dr Logan commented, 'but one thing's clear: interestingly, the coin doesn't seem to be able to take a hold on her. Nor Titch. That's probably how it works with animals.'

'Do you think it only affects humans then?' Molly asked.

'Well, that's a question. To be sure, maybe . . . maybe I should touch it.' Dr Logan rubbed his forehead. Everyone looked appalled. 'Just for a second,' he assured them. 'It won't "take" immediately. Remember, Molly, Fritha said it needed a minute or so. I'll just hold it for ten seconds.'

Molly, Rocky, Gerry and Toka all hesitated.

'If I don't, we won't know for certain that it works,' Dr Logan insisted. He took off his glasses and rubbed his eyes.

'That's true,' Rocky said.

Cautiously the old man reached his hand towards the pouch.

'Immense pull it has!' he said. 'I'll pick it up for a few seconds.' His fingers closed about the coin. 'Mmm. Interesting. Calming. Mmm.' He dropped his glasses. They clattered to the floor.

'Put it down!' Molly said sternly.

Her grandfather looked lazily up at her. 'Down, down, down to the bottom of the sea,' he said, in a sing-song way, pulling the coin towards him.

'LET GO OF IT, GRANDPA!' Molly shouted.

Dr Logan smiled oddly at her, gripping the coin tighter.

There was nothing for it. Molly grabbed at the coin. As her fingers touched it, it gave her a sharp shock. 'OW! DR LOGAN, PUT THE COIN DOWN!'

At once Dr Logan's eyes opened wide and, shaking his hand wildly, he dropped the coin. 'Get away from me!' he said. 'I am not your master!'

Petula dived forward and snapped the coin up in her mouth.

'My goodness!' Dr Logan exclaimed, recovering. 'That was quite the most relaxed I've ever felt! I dropped my spectacles, but, more than that, I felt like dropping everything.' He laughed. 'Does it work? It most certainly does. If we get that into Proila's hands, why, things will go swimmingly!'

Molly grimaced. 'Wow! That hurt!'

Gerry laughed and clapped. 'Bad luck, Molly! But brilliant! It works! So how and when do we get it to Proila?'

'He's playing the Tokyo Dome again tonight,' Toka said. He picked up a cardboard box from the side of the room. 'Luckily we are ready, and well prepared.' Out of the box he pulled six pairs of earphones. 'We bought earplugs too!'

'What time will he be onstage?' Molly asked.

'Eight thirty.'

'We should arrive at eight fifty,' Molly decided. 'Then his set will definitely have started. You guys can go into the building through the main entrance, but Dr Logan and I shouldn't. If his guards see me, I'm dead.'

'So what's the plan?' Gerry asked.

'Well,' Molly pondered, 'I think the stage is the best place for me to confront him.'

'I agree,' said Rocky. 'Otherwise he will just try to force you to give him the coin – even if it does give him a shock when he tries to take it. In front of all his new fans, he's more likely to want to appear charming.'

Molly nodded. 'I think a good plan is this: you guys get backstage – remember you should wear the earphones. Toka can get you in, can't you?' Toka nodded enthusiastically. 'Petula and I will stay with Dr Logan in the car, and at, shall we say, eight fifty exactly, we will floom on to the edge of the stage. We won't be able to get right up to Proila as Dr Logan can't get near the music coin.'

'You'll wear earphones?'

'You bet.'

'Then what?' asked Gerry.

'We'll hope he wants the new coin. Petula will help us.' Petula opened her eyes and rubbed her nose with her paw. 'I know it sounds vague, but I think we'll have to play it by ear.'

'And then what?'

'I'm not sure really. We escape, I suppose.'

Chapter Thirty-seven

Four hours later, Molly and her friends were at the Tokyo Dome.

Rocky, Toka and Gerry were inside. Molly, Dr Logan and Petula sat in the car.

Molly stared out of the window, biting her lip. Her insides were a storm of nerves.

Dr Logan patted Molly's hand. 'Feeling all right? From what you've told me, you've had a lot of experience dealing with villainous people. Hopefully you are feeling sure of yourself.'

'Before, my hypnotism kept me sure of myself in dangerous situations,' she confided. 'Now I've lost my skills I'm not sure of myself at all. I feel like I'm about to be thrown into a pit to fight a monster, but I've got no armour and no weapons.'

'Just remember, whatever happens, I'll be there with

the floom. Like a getaway car, it will be, erm . . . revving, I think that is the expression. I won't be able to get near the coin, but if you are in trouble I'll help you get away.'

'What if I'm scared or panicking?' Molly asked. 'Will I be able to concentrate enough to get on the floom?'

'If you focus your mind and keep a hold of yourself, yes.'

'And if I can't?'

'Then just grab hold of me. I'll stick with you, and hopefully we'll find an opportunity to surf away.'

Molly nodded. Her mouth was dry from nerves. She knew that if Mr Proila didn't go for the bait, and if she was too scared to concentrate on flooming, she'd be stuck. Mr Proila would have her taken away. Dr Logan might be able to floom to her, but there was no guarantee that he could. The idea of being chopped up into lots of little pieces and scattered over Japan filled her with fear again.

Fifteen minutes later she tapped her grandfather on the arm. 'Grandpa, are you ready?'

They got out of the car and heard the roar of the crowd inside the stadium.

'Proila's definitely onstage,' Molly said.

She passed her grandfather his earphones and pushed soft wax earplugs into her own ears. She picked up Petula, giving her a good cuddle. She hoped it wouldn't be the last time she'd kiss her pug's velvety ears. She clutched the pouch with the do-nothing coin in it and shut her eyes.

Almost at once they were moving. Molly opened her eyes. Straight through the arena's thick walls they went, straight through the thousands of people in the auditorium.

Molly saw Mr Proila. He was onstage, dressed in a rhinestone-studded jumpsuit and high-heeled boots, with guitars and banjos on stands all around him. He was clutching the music coin and seemed to be playing a mouth organ, but it was music that neither Molly nor her grandfather could hear.

Dr Logan brought them right up to the stage, as near to Mr Proila as he was able. As the floom was still activated, no one could see them. Molly looked into the audience. She recognized one face from the newspapers: the Prime Minister of Japan.

'I wish I could just jump off and hypnotize him for you, Molly,' Dr Logan said, 'but I'm not as good as I was and, anyway, you know the music coin won't allow me close.'

Molly nodded. Then, holding Petula tight, she stepped off the floom.

The audience gasped. It was as if Molly and Petula had been spun out of thin air. Molly put Petula down on to the stage.

Mr Proila stopped playing the mouth organ. In fact, he stepped back in surprise and knocked a banjo off its stand.

The audience recognized Molly at once. They were still hooked on her. They loved her. And so they began to clap and cheer wildly.

Wasting no time, Molly swung towards Mr Proila and held up the pouch. Girding herself with a courage that was paper-thin, she unfastened the pouch. Turning it inside out so that it fitted her hand like a mitten, she exposed the coin, her fingers gripping it through the leather.

Mr Proila stood and stared. He'd been stunned by Molly's sudden appearance and now he was utterly perplexed by her behaviour. He looked at the coin she held up. It glittered under the stage lights. He read Molly's lips.

'Look, Mr Proila, I've got an amazing coin! With it I can appear and disappear and travel through space and time. And play wonderful music. You thought that you'd beaten me, but, sorry, this coin is far superior to yours. I have BEATEN YOU!'

Mr Proila gulped as a lightning-fast series of thoughts flew through his head.

Firstly, his instinct told him that this Moon girl's new coin was better than his. Secondly, it occurred to him that this meant that the Moon girl was now incredibly dangerous to him.

Greed got the better of him. Mr Proila could already feel the new coin's power. He knew he must have it before Molly whizzed off anywhere. He switched off his microphone. His hand shot out. He grabbed at the new coin.

'Thank you so much!' he exclaimed. His laughing voice was now inaudible to the crowd. 'You stupid child! Now I have both coins. You'll have to show me how it works later, but for now it's on with the sh . . .' Mr Proila was about to fling his arms out in exhilaration – to momentarily hold both coins up to the lights in a gesture of victory – but he stopped. The effort was too much, he thought. He felt fabulous enough without gloating. 'Yes . . . yes. On with the shhhh . . .' he said with a smile.

He dropped down on his knees and looked at the amazing new coin in his hand. The very energy inside him seemed to flow more steadily around his body because of it. He could feel his blood moving down his legs and up the other side of him as though it was a magical, life-giving sap that he had never noticed before. His feet felt heavy and grounded, like the roots of a tree. In fact, his legs felt like the trunk of a tree, his body and arms its leafy branches – his head a mass of blossom. And then, the heaviness of this feeling started to grow lighter and lighter. The blossom of his mind felt as if it was blowing away. The audience was clapping and he was floating . . . floating away.

All that Mr Proila could feel that had any weight to it now was the new coin he had taken from the girl – that girl whose name he couldn't remember. The coin with its circle marked in the centre of it. Or was it a zero? A nothing?

Molly watched hopefully as Mr Proila's countenance changed. She willed the new coin to do its work. Mr Proila's expression dropped from angry and authoritative to dreamy. The hand holding the new coin grasped it tighter and tighter while the hand with the old coin in it grew looser and looser.

And then the music coin fell. To Molly, it was as if

it was falling in slow motion, for so many conflicting thoughts raced through her mind as it dropped.

'It's mine! Mine again at last!' one part of Molly delighted.

Then another part of her snapped, 'No! It's never to be yours again. Leave it.'

A third urged, 'If you pick it up and use it one last time, you can fix all the bad stuff that Mr Proila has done. And there's an audience out there. Mr Proila's bodyguards too. What are you going to do about them?'

As the music coin dropped on to the stage and rolled across the ground, Mr Proila slumped down. Molly's eyes lifted and engaged with the audience. She picked up Mr Proila's electric guitar and spoke into the microphone.

'HELLO, TOKYO!' she shouted. 'It seems Proila is a bit tired!'

The audience laughed, thinking Mr Proila's exhaustion and his sitting on the stage was some sort of act.

'So,' Molly went on, gesturing to Dr Logan at the side of the stage, 'I'd like you to meet my great-great-grandfather.' The audience laughed again, as of course this was a joke – no one's great-great-grandfather was alive.

Molly stepped up to the music coin, lying where Mr Proila had dropped it, and pressed her foot on it. Immediately she could feel its power as it tried to commune with her again. Like an evil spirit it wanted its power over her back.

Petula watched Molly, unsure what was happening.

'Molly! Leave the coin!' she barked.

'What are you doing, Molly?' Dr Logan called anxiously from the edge of the stage. He held his earphones firmly in place, for he was suspicious about what Molly was planning to do.

'Don't worry!' Molly reassured them both. Then she did something that completely horrified him and Petula and Toka, Gerry and Rocky, who were observing from the wings. Molly picked up the music coin and put it in her pocket! Taking a white electric guitar, she began to play.

Petula took hold of Molly's trousers in her teeth and she began to tug.

But Molly played. And she played more brilliantly than ever before. Gerry, Rocky and Toka watched helplessly from the side of the stage, their attempts to push past a guard unsuccessful.

The audience stood in awe – many with their mouths hanging open. Molly's music was far superior to Proila's. His had been good. But Molly's was heavenly.

The crowd would have been amazed at what was really going on in Molly's head.

Molly wasn't thinking anything at all about the music she was playing. It was imperative that she didn't. Instead Molly had filled her mind with something else – the word that Do had taught her: AUM. AUM filled her mind from back to front, from side to side, and top to bottom just as Do had suggested it might be able to. It blocked out everything else. So while Molly's hands played on

257

automatic, doing the music coin's bidding, her mind was protected. She didn't even hear – not a note – and so she was not a slave to the coin. Molly was taking the coin's power without it taking hers. Her fingers held down frets and strummed and picked on strings, working a musical frenzy on the instrument. And the music she made ensnared her audience, but it had absolutely no effect on her.

When she'd finished, the audience exploded.

Molly reached her hand into the pocket and took the coin out. She bowed to the audience and as she bent lower, as if to pat Petula, she gave the coin to her dog. 'You look after this now,' she whispered. She nodded to Dr Logan and smiled at her friends in the wings, who she could see were watching her with wide, terrified eyes.

Then Molly's eyes sought out the prime minister. There he was, applauding enthusiastically. When she caught his eye, the prime minister even put two fingers to his mouth and whistled shrilly. Molly held her hand up to the audience. Immediately it fell silent.

'Thank you,' Molly said. 'Glad you liked the show. Now I have something serious to talk to you about. So, if you don't mind, please will you listen for a few minutes.' Molly glanced over at Gerry and made a thumbs-up signal to him. She beckoned at Toka, who came and translated her words into Japanese. 'I think a lot of you will know that some strange new laws have been passed in Japan. Whale hunting has been made legal again. So have dogfighting and cockfighting. I am sure that many of you think this is wrong.'

The audience murmured and a few shouts of agreement rang through the arena.

Now Molly spoke directly to the prime minister, who was staring at her adoringly. 'Mr Prime Minister, I know that you and your cabinet have recently been persuaded to change these laws – but please, for all the animals, and for the Japanese people, and the people of the world, and for me, please will you change the laws back?'

Molly stepped up to the VIP box and she thrust the mic towards the politician. She hoped that the brief burst of music she had played had been enough to affect him.

The Prime Minister of Japan bent his head closer to the microphone. 'Of course,' he agreed. And he put his hand out to Molly to shake on the promise.

Chapter Thirty-eight

After lots of bowing to the enthralled audience, Molly and Dr Logan helped Mr Proila to his feet. They bent him over, helping him to bow too. The audience laughed, assuming it was a comedy act. They cheered as Molly and the old man led Mr Proila off the stage. Petula followed, with the music coin safely in her mouth.

Backstage, Gerry, Rocky and Toka were waiting.

'How did you do it, Molly?' Rocky asked. 'How did you resist the coin?'

'By not letting the thought of it into my head,' Molly said. 'It's a trick Do taught me.'

'The whales will be so happy,' Gerry said, hugging Molly around the waist.

'Well, after the trouble I caused, Gerry, there was some fixing to do.'

'The trouble *I* caused, you mean,' Dr Logan said.

'Petula's doing an excellent job of being its guardian now.'

Petula wagged her tail and Molly bent down to give her a stroke. 'Good girl, Petula.'

Now everyone's attention fell on Mr Proila.

'So what do we do with him?' Toka asked. 'He's good for nothing.'

'That's because he's got the do-nothing coin!' Gerry laughed. His hat bobbed about as Titch ran about in its lining.

Rocky touched Mr Proila's arm. 'Wow,' he gasped. 'He gives off a sort of relaxed vibe.'

'We don't want him losing that coin,' Toka said.

Mr Proila's hand was clamped vice-like around the do-nothing coin, in contrast to the rest of him, which was as floppy as a jelly.

'He needs to be somewhere where he's watched,' Toka said.

'How about takin' him to the old monk you met?' Gerry suggested.

'I could take him now,' Dr Logan said. 'In the state he's in he's the perfect passenger. I've carried hypnotized people before. The board seems to accept them as under my power. Once he's at Do's monastery, everyone's safer.'

Everyone agreed that this was a great plan.

'But poor Do,' Gerry said, 'havin' to look after this lump.'

'He won't mind,' Molly reassured Gerry. 'He'll see it as a Zen challenge.'

Molly gave her great-great-grandfather a big hug.

'Thanks. Thanks not just for this but for everything. Without you I never could have sorted this all out. And after this you deserve a big rest. You look so tired, Grandpa.'

Dr Logan did a funny little salute, then he took his floom in his fingers and he put his hand on Mr Proila's shoulder. He shut his eyes.

In the next second, there was a hiss as they shrank and disappeared.

'Wow!' Gerry said. 'If everyone had one of those disc things, we wouldn't need planes!'

'Cool guy,' Toka declared.

'Now,' Rocky said, 'we need to decide what to do with the music coin.'

'Petula could look after it,' Gerry suggested. 'Although that wouldn't really be fair. I don't 'spect it tastes that nice.' He took Titch out of his hat to let him see what was going on.

'We could bury it under a mountain or throw it into the deepest part of the sea,' Rocky suggested.

Molly's eyes lit up.

The perfect solution involved, first of all, arranging to meet Hiroyuki, Chokichi and Miss Sny and telling them everything that had happened. They of course needed some decompressing from the hypnotic music that Mr Proila had played to them, but that wasn't difficult. With earphones on himself, Rocky played them a recording of Molly's music. Though Molly no longer possessed the coin, her music from that time had the strength to cancel out the power of Mr Proila's.

Then Miss Sny arranged for a limo to drive them all to the fishing village of Nakaminato.

A small but comfortable fishing ship awaited them. It had enough berths for everyone. But more important was that the crew was friendly and, crucially, whale loving. In fact, the captain, a thickset moustached man, had a special interest in whales. In his cabin he had albums full of photographs that he had taken of whales throughout his long years at sea.

There was also a cabin full of radar equipment and devices to locate whales, and recording equipment that the captain could let down into the water to film the creatures and listen to the amazing sounds they made.

'It was very disturbing when hunting whales was made legal,' he said as everyone crowded into his cabin. 'I am probably the happiest man in Japan today, knowing that the prime minister has banned whale hunting again.'

Gerry looked admiringly at the captain. 'What a nice job you've got.'

The journey was an easy one as the sea was calm. And the next morning, after a good night's sleep, everyone gathered on deck. Sunlight poured down on them and the sea flashed silver, reflecting the sky. It stretched for miles, water in every direction.

'They are near,' the captain said. 'It looks empty, but the whales are there.'

Molly found that her heart was beating fast. Were

they under the boat, or a mile off?

And then they appeared. First it was just a glimpse – the glint of a wet whale back, the tip of a tail surfacing and catching the sun. There was a massive noise – a *PAH* on the other side of the ship that broke the hush of the sea. It was the unmistakable sound of life – giant life – giant ocean life. It was the noise of a massive animal in the sea, an animal with lungs the size of trees, surfacing and letting out a breath and taking in another. It was a sound like Molly had never heard before.

Everyone ran to that side of the ship.

'One, two, three,' Gerry counted. 'Look! Four, five, six, seven! Seven of them! Look! Two babies! And those ones are teenagery whales. That one's a giant!'

'He must be the dad,' Rocky said.

Everyone was thrilled and overwhelmed by the wonderful sight.

The whales rolled and played in the water, their huge bodies grey and wet, the sea as comfortable to them as air to a human. And then they were off. They began swimming away, in a line. Like a Mexican wave, their bodies came up and went down, almost as if each one was connected to the next.

The engines started. Soon the ship was travelling with the whales on either side of it. When the whales slowed down and began to play again, the ship stopped too. Molly looked over the edge.

A huge whale was swimming beneath the boat. And then an amazing thing happened. This giant whale came up, rising like a gentle monster from the deep. It surfaced right beside the ship, water spraying from its blowhole – showering everyone watching. It was an exhilarating moment, half scary to be near such a powerful creature, half exciting and totally awe-inspiring.

Petula barked at Molly. Oddly, her bark didn't sound like an ordinary bark. It sounded more like the tooting of a flute.

'Wow! That sounded cool,' Molly said. Then, 'Yes!' she agreed, knowing exactly what Petula wanted to do. 'Give it to him!' Molly held Petula up and held her over the edge of the ship. Petula positioned herself and then, with a toss of her head, she threw the music coin into the sea.

At once the coin sank, dropping down through the water on to the bull whale. The whale dived down, taking the coin with it.

'Captain,' Molly said urgently, 'can we go to your cabin and watch the whales through your cameras?'

'Certainly. Come with me.'

With the press of a few buttons, the equipment was switched on. And out of the speakers in the recording cabin came the most extraordinary sound. It was of a bull whale singing.

'That is quite extraordinary,' the captain said, twiddling knobs to check his machinery was working properly. 'I've never, ever heard a whale sing as wonderfully as that. It seems to be splitting its voice into two and harmonizing! It's completely . . . mesmerizing! I must record this.' He pressed a button.

Molly gave Gerry a wink.

'When you've recorded him,' Gerry suggested, 'you can sell the CD. And the money you make can help save the whales and protect the seas everywhere in the world.'

Molly picked up Petula and hugged her. She carried her out on to the deck. And from there they watched the pod of whales as they Mexican-waved away.

Chapter Thirty-nine

That afternoon they all returned to Tokyo. They were salty-faced and windswept from their brilliant time whale watching.

When they got back to the apartment, Do was waiting for them there, looking very out of place in his simple monk's clothes. Everyone looked at him in surprise.

'Has Mr Proila escaped?' Molly blurted out.

Do got up. 'Oh no, Molly. He fine. He like sloth. He stay there like pet until I return.'

'I'm sorry, Do. I thought you wouldn't mind having him,' Molly said, walking towards him. 'Do you not want him there?' she asked anxiously. 'Is that the thing? I can completely see why you wouldn't.'

The monk shook his head. 'No! No, I like him. He remind me how to be still. Good inspiration.' His smile dropped.

All the children came and gathered around the monk.

'Have you come to say goodbye?' Molly guessed. 'You know, Do, I never would have gone back home without coming to see you again.' Molly smiled.

Do sighed. 'I know. But I have to bring you something.'

He pulled a small bag out of his pocket and gave it to Molly. She opened it. Inside were four things. A clear time-stop crystal. A green crystal. A red crystal. And her great-great-grandfather's floom.

'He wanted you to have them,' Do said.

Molly paused, confused. 'But . . . but he can't give me this.' She picked out the red gem. 'He'll never get back to his own time without this.'

'No.' Do shook his head. 'He won't.'

Molly looked at Do's peaceful face.

'He wanted you to have these. He told me to tell you that meeting you was one of the greatest pleasures of his life.'

'Where's he gone?' Yet even as these words left Molly's lips she knew the answer.

'The question of what happens after life is question that unifies human beings.' Do sighed again, his chest giving a slow heave up and then down. 'I don't know the answer.'

Molly was stunned. 'I can't believe it . . .' she whispered.

'He very old, Molly. His spirit strong but his body weak. It run out of power. He conk out. I'm sorry for you.'

Molly shook her head and held the precious bag tight.

'I wish . . .' she murmured. 'Oh, I wish I'd got to know him better.'

Everyone was quiet.

Do broke the silence. 'Now you come upstairs. I have good surprise for you.'

Molly nodded and she and the others followed the monk out of the apartment and up in the lift to the roof garden.

There a lovely sight greeted them. The trees on the roof had all burst into blossom. White blossom.

'They're all boffed up!' Gerry shouted.

'It like six white clouds living on our roof!' Toka exclaimed.

'All over Japan, blossom start,' Do said. 'Look, see in park!'

The children peered out beyond the roof terrace and saw that, indeed, the park a few blocks away was full of blossom trees. Pink ones and white ones.

'It's like candyfloss!' Gerry said.

'That cherry blossom. And see people having picnics?' Hiroyuki pointed out. 'Now the season of *hanami*, of celebrating blossom. Everyone celebrate life.'

There was blossom everywhere. On rooftops, on balconies, in small triangles of grass in the city and in the parks.

Do sat cross-legged beneath one of the trees. 'This white blossom my favourite. It blossom with big beauty, but only for a week. Then blossom blow away. It remind me of life. So beautiful . . . then suddenly gone.'

Molly sat down beside him. 'Thank you for bringing Dr Logan's things, Do. But . . . but what about his . . . his body?'

Do nodded. 'He ask me to cremate body. I did.' The old monk dipped his hand into his bag and passed Molly a green porcelain urn. 'These are Dr Logan ashes.'

Rocky sat down beside Molly and put a hand on her shoulder. 'That's really cool, Molly. We can take them back to Briersville and scatter his ashes there.'

'Yes,' Do agreed. 'Like blossom blowing away on the wind, he will go.'

Tickets were bought for Molly, Petula, Rocky and Gerry to travel back home.

It was arranged that Miss Sny was to be left in charge of Chokichi and Hiroyuki's music careers until Mr Proila returned, which everyone knew was going to be never.

On the day that Molly and her friends were due to leave, they finally met the boys' parents. They were all going to live together again, with Miss Sny.

As Molly, Rocky, Petula and Gerry drove away, the boys' mother was making lunch in the kitchen, and their father was playing a Japanese board game with all three of his sons. The old grandmother was painting the missing eyes on to her strange dolls. All the wishes she had made had evidently been granted.

As they boarded the plane, Molly realized how lonely she had been when she'd lost all the people she loved in her life. She realized how fabulous it was that they had cared so much for her that, even when she was a monster, they had wanted to help her.

Molly knew she could be a monster again – a mini-monster, cross about something or bad-tempered or angry – and her friends and family would be horrible sometimes too. But she knew for certain that underneath, however grumpy the people in her family might be, they actually all cared about each other.

Molly saw clearly how amazing and brilliant and lucky this was. And she knew too, from losing her great-great-grandfather, how she must try from now on to appreciate the people about her. For, in Do's words, they might just 'conk out'. Then it would be too late to show them how much they were appreciated.

Part of Molly was sad that she had lost her powers. But oddly she was also half pleased that they had gone. Without them life was more of a challenge. She would be a regular person now, someone without incredible hypnotic skills, someone who couldn't hypnotize people with the flash of an eye, who couldn't time travel, or mind read or morph.

She recognized that her greatest pleasures in life came from her friends and her family. She didn't need the hypnotic arts to make this better.

But the greatest lesson that Molly had learned in her time in Japan was about badness. She saw how bad deeds not only hurt the people they were aimed at, they also hurt the person doing them. And it had become obvious to her that the more bad things a person does, the more their character becomes bad. A pinch of it here, a ladleful there, the badness mounts up until it starts to mould the person. The person becomes what they do.

Molly saw that it was all about choice. A person who does good things glows with goodness because they have chosen good things. You are what you do, Molly thought.

She watched Rocky helping Gerry open a packet of crayons.

'You are what you do . . .' she said under her breath.

She looked out of the window at the earth below and thought of the billions of people living on it. The billions of people of the world living, breathing, each one being who they were because of what they did, each one affecting the world and each other by their actions. As though a mass of voices was whispering to her inside her head, a bigger thought came to Molly:

'We are what we do.'

Dear Reader

Our oceans are in trouble.

Human beings have dirtied the seas and killed marine life. There are fewer and fewer fish. Imagine the seas empty.

There are seven billion people on this planet. If every person made an effort to look after our oceans we could put things right again.

We need underwater national parks. We need to keep our seas clean. We need to stop trawlers raking the bottom of the seas to catch fish, killing everything that their rakes scrape over. We need to let the fish grow big enough to have little fish.

If we eat fish, we need to make very sure it is from waters where there are enough fish, and that they are caught properly. We need to make a fuss and ask about these things in the shops where we buy fish.

Gerry says: 'I'm sick of watching adults messing things up.'

If the five billion adults on the planet can't sort things out, maybe they need some help from the two billion children.

Please try to get the people around you to wake up and think about preserving our oceans and the marine life in them.

Thank you for your help.

Love from
Georgia Byng

Rocky's Song

Hypnotize yourself to believe you can.
Mesmerize the world to better its plan.
Hypnotize for good and never with badness.
Bring on the peace and wipe out the sadness.

Acknowledgements

To my patient editor, Polly Nolan, for her brilliant notes and for writing 'PACE!' on the page whenever the book was getting boring.

Polly's cuts were perfect and her thoughts on everything from plot to characters very much appreciated.

The other thank you is to Caradoc King, who couldn't be a better agent. He is clever and well read, kind and supportive. He is also a very good writer. His own book about his early life is the most moving account of a childhood that I have ever read.

Georgia Byng

MOLLY MOON

and the
Morphing Mystery

Molly Moon is unstoppable!

Soon she and her brother, Micky, are swapping bodies with ladybirds, dogs, rats, even the Queen of England herself! But the fun can't last forever. If they don't find the world's only copy of *The Advanced Arts of Hypnotism* they'll never get back into their own bodies. And it doesn't help that they are being sabotaged by a very strange group of people intent on destroying the world . . and the weather is behaving VERY oddly indeed.

Collect them all!